WITCH IN CHARGE

A BLAIR WITCH MYSTERY

ELLE ADAMS

1

———

obody told me he'd bring the dragon to work with him.

Of all the times for a baby dragon to get loose in the office, it had to happen at the very end of the last day of work, before I left town for a week. My co-workers and I surrounded the desk, forming a barrier around the reptilian creature in a desperate attempt to stop it from setting any of the records ablaze. When we'd accepted a client's request to help him find an assistant with the skills to handle his rare magical beasts, we hadn't expected him to actually *bring* one of them to our office. Even at Eldritch & Co, Fairy Falls's only magical recruitment agency, this was a new one.

Worse, in less than an hour, I was supposed to be meeting up with Rebecca, the Head Witch of the northwest of England, and at this rate, I'd be a no-show because I was too busy putting out fires—literally.

The dragon opened its maw. Bethan, the boss's daughter, waved her wand and cast a protective spell on the four computers sitting on our shared office desk the instant before the dragon spat out a mouthful of fire. Lizzie leapt in, casting a bubble spell that doused the flames and left the desks untouched. The ends of her frizzy hair were singed from when she'd jumped in to save the printer from a close encounter with a fireball earlier. My own magic wasn't exactly at its best while I was under stress, but it was Rob who was at a distinct disadvantage. The blond werewolf couldn't use magic himself, but instead of retreating out of harm's way, as we'd advised him to, he kept trying to talk soothingly to our scaly guest without much success.

"Come on. You don't want to stay here in the office," he murmured to the dragon. "You want to go outside, right? If you get back in your cage, your owner will be able to get you out of here."

The owner in question was helpfully hiding in the reception area with Callie, our exasperated werewolf receptionist and Rob's cousin. I didn't blame the dragon for looking sceptical and refusing to budge from the desk, but when it spat out another mouthful of flames, we had to move fast to prevent our books and papers from catching ablaze. I flicked my wand and conjured up a cloud of raindrops, accidentally drenching half the desk in the process.

"Oops." I looked sheepishly at the damp pile of paperwork. "Sorry, everyone."

"It's okay. We can just print it again," said Bethan. "I doubt he's going back in that cage by choice. That leaves us with two options: use a sleeping spell or open the window."

"Why the window?" asked Lizzie, casting another shielding spell on the coffee machine before the dragon's fire set it alight. "To let it outside?"

I raised a brow at Bethan. "You want to risk it flying away?"

"That would be its owner's problem and not ours," said Bethan. "He hasn't exactly come to give us a hand, has he?"

"True." I ducked under a stray fireball and waved my wand, accidentally making it rain glitter all over the desk. "Sleeping spells are harmless enough, so I think we should try that route first."

Taking our target by surprise was easier said than done. Every time one of us pointed our wand at the dragon, another jet of flame appeared and forced us to pivot to protect our office from catching fire. The temptation seized me to just open the window and let the owner deal with the problem, but the beast wasn't trained in the slightest, and it might throw a fireball at some innocent bystander if we let it outside. We couldn't take the risk.

"I'll cast the spell," Bethan offered. "Lizzie and Blair, distract its attention. Rob... keep talking to it."

"I don't think it's a fan of my stories," Rob remarked. "I'll try, though."

Lizzie and I moved to stand in front of the printer and the coffee machine and raised our wands, drawing the dragon's attention, while Bethan slipped around the desk from behind. As Rob talked soothingly in the dragon's ear, Bethan raised her wand and pointed it at her target.

The dragon reared up and unleashed a jet of flame, its biggest yet, spraying everything in the vicinity. Lizzie and I waved our wands, but we couldn't stop a patch of carpet catching fire. I jumped to put it out, missing the moment when the sleeping spell hit the dragon from behind. It yelped, reared up again—and keeled over.

At that moment, my boss, Veronica, pushed open the office door. "Oh, good, you've got it under control."

Bethan—who looked almost exactly like her mother except with brown hair instead of white—ran to catch the dragon's unconscious body before it fell off the desk. "If you don't count the fires."

"Yeah. Those." I prodded the still-smoking piece of carpet out with my wand and allowed myself a moment of relief that I'd managed to spare most of our paperwork. "Is the owner ready to come back and collect his beastie?"

"I believe he ran outside."

Bethan swore under her breath, lifted the dragon into its cage, and then closed the hatch. "Seriously? We're not keeping this in the office."

"I'm sure we'll be able to convince him to come back," said Veronica. "Then we might be able to find him an assistant."

"Absolutely not." Bethan lifted her head. "Do you think anyone in their right mind would want to work with that guy? Besides, we were supposed to go home ten minutes ago."

Ten minutes? Oh no. I was already late to meet Rebecca.

Veronica wore a wistful expression. "It's always a shame when a client doesn't work out, isn't it?"

The four of us exchanged raised eyebrows, taking in the slightly damp and singed office around us. Then I cleared my throat. "Ah, Veronica, I'm sorry to leave at a time like this, but I have a meeting at the witches' headquarters—"

"You can go, Blair," she said. "I know you have a big day tomorrow."

I felt bad for leaving the others to clean up the mess, but I might have another emergency on my hands if I didn't make it to the witches' headquarters before Rebecca picked up her exam results. Taking responsibility for a highly strung tween witch who also happened to be the most powerful witch in the region was not for the faint of heart.

After waving goodbye to the others, I left work and sprinted down the road towards the witches' headquarters. It gave me a jolt of mild horror to see none other than

Madame Grey herself standing outside the tall oak doors to the grand house, waiting for me. The leader of the Meadowsweet Coven watched calmly as I stopped to catch my breath, looking as formidable as ever in her grey robes and silver-rimmed spectacles. Her hair, a brilliant shade of white, was pulled into a bun behind her head.

"Sorry," I gasped out. "Had to deal with an emergency situation at work. I'm not too late, am I?"

"Rebecca already has her results."

My heart dropped. "Oh."

"Don't look so worried."

"It's good news?" I lifted my head. "Please tell me it's good news."

"Ask her yourself," she said. "In the meantime, I believe Veronica is in need of my assistance in finding the owner of a certain reptile."

She stepped aside to let me enter the witches' headquarters, leaving me wondering how on earth she'd found out about that. Veronica must have called her, which at least meant my co-workers might actually get to go home tonight after all. That was one bit of good news already.

After pushing open the doors, I ran through the lobby of the witches' headquarters towards the classroom we used for our magic lessons. Through the window, I saw Rebecca sitting at her usual desk near the front of the room, her cat familiar curled up at her feet. Our mutual tutor, Rita, raised her brows at me when I pushed open the classroom door.

"Rebecca." I halted in the doorway. "Sorry I'm late. A baby dragon nearly set my office on fire. How'd it go?"

The tall, slender young witch held up the paper in answer, beaming at me. My gaze danced all over the pace before it settled on her scores. *Perfect.*

"I can't believe it," she said, lowering the paper. "Can you?"

"I can." I grinned. "Told you it'd be fine."

"You did," she said. "Sorry I spent so much of our lesson time fretting."

"Don't apologise." Rebecca had unexpectedly gained the title of Head Witch for the region at the age of only eleven, and I didn't blame her for feeling under pressure to perform at her best in every way. She'd also had an extra challenge in that she'd had to learn to cast every spell with both her regular wand and her sceptre—a long, pointed stick that served as proof of her Head Witch status—which was currently propped against her chair next to her sleeping familiar.

"Blair, in case you've forgotten, you also have some exam results ready to collect."

Oh boy.

In a jingle of bangles, Rita pushed another piece of paper into my hands, which showed my scores on the exams I'd taken the previous week. My gaze skimmed down the page—and then I stared at the numbers, disbelieving. I'd got full marks on my latest theory exam *and* the practical one too.

"How?" I blurted. "How did that happen?"

Had the examiner taken pity on me? *No way.* That wasn't allowed, and besides, my exam papers had been marked by someone who hadn't a clue who I was.

"How else?" asked Rita. "You worked hard and were rewarded for your efforts."

I gaped at her, unable to believe that all the late nights of studying and juggling magic lessons with work and everything else in my madcap life had actually paid off. "I... wow. Thank you. Honestly, this is more on you than on me."

Rita had tutored me from the very beginning of my induction into the magical world, and it was under her tuition that I'd gone from a clueless newbie witch who didn't even know which hand to hold her wand in to passing my exams with flying colours. It seemed impossible, but the numbers on the page didn't lie.

"Don't be absurd," she said. "This is a result of your hard work, make no mistake. Though, the real work will begin when you're back from your meeting. That's when we'll start on Grade Five."

That brought me back down to earth. Grade Five was the magical equivalent to secondary school, which meant that while Rebecca had officially caught up to witches of her own age, I had a long way to go before I reached the average skill of someone older than twelve.

"But... we've already been learning Grade Five spells, haven't we?" Rebecca ventured.

"Yes, we have," Rita agreed. "Unfortunately, there's a limit to what can be taught in a classroom, especially when it comes to the types of magic a Head Witch might be required to have at her disposal."

Rebecca's smile faded. I understood why Rita had reminded her of the challenges still ahead of her, but it would have been nice to have the chance to celebrate her accomplishments first.

"Regardless, you did well," said Rita, as if sensing the dimming mood. "Both of you. Instead of a regular lesson today, I'm going to go through all the spells you might need on your trip to meet the other Head Witches."

Despite her praise, Rita didn't hold back in the slightest, as she had Rebecca and me run through all the useful defensive spells we'd been practising over the past few months. To my surprise, Rita had almost no complaints for either of us, but she had plenty of warnings about what we might face at the upcoming meeting.

One would have thought she expected us to get attacked by the other Head Witches—which, admittedly, wasn't out of the realm of possibility. Every Head Witch who'd be at tomorrow's meeting had countless years more experience than us, though I couldn't help thinking that the most likely threat would be far subtler than someone openly challenging Rebecca for her title of Head Witch and her sceptre.

When the lesson ended, Rebecca left the room with Toast, her familiar, on her heels. I caught up to her in the lobby, where I found her staring listlessly at the paper with her exam results, her expression preoccupied.

"What is it?" I asked.

"According to my exam results, I'm better than any witch my age, but it isn't enough," she mumbled. "I still don't have as much training as the other Head Witches. They're all so much more experienced than I am, and they've been preparing for years."

"We've been preparing too," I said. "Besides, you aren't going to be expected to make any major announcements. Most of the covens' policy-related stuff is pretty much set in stone. All you have to do is smile, nod, and not start any fights."

The Head Witches didn't like change, though, and a tween witch who happened to be the daughter of a convicted criminal joining their ranks was disruptive enough that some of them might raise a fuss, even if Rebecca sat in the corner and said nothing. I wished there were a way to skip over this meeting altogether, but that might cause even more of a scandal. There was no winning with some people.

"They're still more accomplished than I am," she said.

"One of them actually invented three new potions. Another cured a magical disease. What have I done?"

"Don't forget the only requirement for the job is to be chosen by a sceptre," I told her. "I doubt the sceptre looks at people's exam results or achievements before picking someone. Not everyone will have a long list of accomplishments."

"No, but they've had years of practise."

"Even years of experience isn't always enough to prove your capabilities," I said. "I met a wizard today who was supposed to be an expert on magical beasts, and yet he still ran away when his pet baby dragon got loose in our office."

I wasn't sure that would reassure her, but I was way out of my depth too. Without my having a sceptre, it'd be a miracle if I was even allowed into the meeting at all, but I'd do my best to keep any of the other witches from making trouble for her. Madame Grey would be there, too, but she had to keep up a public appearance as the head of our town's witches and was therefore limited in her ways to intervene if things went south. That left it up to me, and I wasn't a Head Witch *or* a coven leader, despite being the only living member of my birth coven.

"I guess." Rebecca lowered her gaze from the paper and followed me to the oak doors leading out of the witches' headquarters.

"Blair."

The sound of my name brought me to a startled halt. Blythe, Rebecca's sister and my former co-worker, waited outside the building, wearing her usual expression of mild distaste.

"Blythe. This is a surprise." I kept my tone polite. While Blythe and I weren't mortal enemies any longer, and we'd had to join forces out of necessity against her scheming mother, that didn't mean she was ever going to be my best friend. And the fact that she could sometimes read my thoughts made it impossible to hide.

"I passed with top marks," Rebecca told her sister before things could get any more awkward. "Is that what you wanted to ask me?"

"I'm coming," Blythe announced, ignoring her sister's announcement entirely, "to meet the other Head Witches."

I frowned. "You are?"

She nodded. "Yes. I know I won't be allowed into the actual meeting, but I want to keep an eye on things."

"Oh." I exchanged perplexed looks with Rebecca. "That's why Madame Grey is going. And... well, me."

When Rebecca had been chosen as Head Witch, I'd been the one who'd offered to help her and not Blythe. I hadn't thought Blythe was paying more than a superficial level of attention to her sister's training.

"I'm her sister," said Blythe. "Look, it doesn't matter how many of us are there. The more, the better."

"Why?" I asked. "I mean, is there a particular reason you think we'll all be needed?"

Their mother was in jail, under the highest possible security, for conspiring against the covens—but if any of the people at the meeting had been her allies, then Blythe would certainly know. *Is there something she's not telling us?*

"No," she said. "You can go home, Blair. I'll see you tomorrow."

"But—" Maybe I was being paranoid. For all I knew, she wanted a sibling heart-to-heart that didn't involve me. "If you're sure. Bye, Rebecca."

I did need to clear up a few things at home before I left town, but I started off by heading towards the woods instead. As a fairy, my dad wouldn't be allowed near the meeting, so I'd promised to keep him updated. Despite the peaceful sounds of birdsong that greeted me upon entering the forest, my nerves jangled at the reminder of Blythe's unexpected appearance. We both had good reason to be paranoid, but she was the one who'd grown up surrounded by her mother's scheming. If she knew of anyone at the meeting who might be out to get us, she'd at least tell Madame Grey, right?

Putting the thought out of mind, with difficulty, I found my way to the semi-transparent path that led from the regular woods into the slightly more otherworldly area where the fairies made their home. From there, I walked to my dad's cottage, which sat in a clearing surrounded by bright flowers. He more than deserved to live in an idyllic setting like this after suffering years in jail for a crime he hadn't committed.

My dad answered the door when I knocked, his pointed face wearing an expression of concern. "How'd it go?"

"I don't know how, but I passed with full marks. So did Rebecca."

This was a novelty to me. At school, I'd always passed my exams, but I'd never been a high achiever. The same had held true when I'd entered the magical world, and the bumpy ride I'd endured since then sometimes made it hard to see how far I'd really come.

A relieved grin broke out on his face. "That's great news. You've worked hard enough to deserve a win."

"I guess I have," I said. "I'm leaving first thing tomorrow for the meeting."

"You think you're ready?"

I shrugged. "Bit late if I'm not. Rebecca has more reason to be worried than I do."

"I'm sure it'll be fine," he said. "I should let you go. You need to pack, don't you? And say goodbye to your friends."

Yeah. Alissa, my flatmate, would still be at work, but I had a date with Nathan at the local pub that evening. "I do. I'll be back before you know it."

After I'd left my dad's house, I walked straight to the Troll's Tavern to meet Nathan. He bought me a specially themed cocktail to celebrate my results, though I firmly declined a glass of wine. Experience told me that wasn't a good idea, and I had to be up early the next day.

"Blythe showed up?" His brows rose when I told him about my other surprise of the evening. "Really? She wants to come with you?"

"Yeah, and I can see why." I sipped my cocktail, which tasted of fizzy orange juice mixed with marshberries. "Rebecca's her little sister, after all."

"I suppose, but has Blythe ever shown up at council meetings before? Or helped Rebecca in her lessons?"

"I thought the same, but I've no idea how Blythe's mind works." As far as older siblings went, she wasn't the most attentive. The large age gap between them was part of the reason, but most of it was Blythe's less-than-sunny personality. I'd been taking lessons with Rebecca for nearly a year now, except for the private Head Witch lessons she took with Madame Grey, and Blythe rarely showed her face. Maybe it was for the best that she hadn't sat in on our lessons and witnessed all my many failures, but I had to wonder why she'd chosen now to take an interest. "This is going to be awkward. Imagine a road trip with Me, Blythe, and Rebecca. Oh, and Madame Grey as well."

"And me?" He leaned forward in his seat. "I was going to ask you, but I had to wait until I was sure I could get the time off work."

My heart skipped a beat. "You want to come with me?"

His brow arched. "If you don't object."

"Obviously not, but I thought your boss might take issue with you leaving town."

"I'm head of security. This is a security issue. Besides, I have some holiday leave saved up."

"I'm sure you were saving it for a nice trip to the seaside, not for this," I pointed out. "This is not a holiday, by any stretch of the imagination. The scheming Head Witches will kind of ruin the mood, won't they?"

"You won't have to deal with them all the time."

"I don't know about that." Even with Blythe and Madame Grey around, too, I didn't believe for a minute that Rebecca wouldn't need my help with whatever schemes the other witches came up with. "If you really want to come, though, I'm not going to object."

Nathan and I had been together for nearly a year, though with everything we'd faced together since my arrival in town, it felt like much longer. I'd hoped for a holiday that didn't involve scheming witches, but at this point, I'd take what I could get.

He reached for my hand under the table. "Was that a yes? Or a no?"

"Sure." I entwined my fingers with his. "I'd be more than happy for you to come with me."

We rarely had time to spend together outside the dates we managed to squeeze into our busy schedules, and this might end up being a drama-free few days that could turn into a relaxing break. Hey, I could dream.

2

We set off early the following morning. As I'd stayed at Nathan's house, I had to stop at home to pick up my suitcase before leaving town, and I found Alissa had just come back from a late shift at the hospital. She sat on the living room sofa with her cat, Roald, curled up on her lap.

"Have fun." She yawned. "As much fun as you can have in the company of a bunch of stuffy Head Witches, that is."

A meowing noise drew my attention to my bedroom, where I found my own cat, Sky, sitting on top of my suitcase.

"Miaow to you too," I said. "You're coming with me, right?"

"Is Sky objecting to you leaving?" asked Alissa from the living room.

"I figured he'd come along. He usually does." Sky might be unpredictable in a lot of ways, but his most dependable trait was that he invited himself everywhere, whether I asked or not. "You didn't think I'd leave you behind, did you?"

"Miaow." He hopped off the suitcase and brushed

against my legs, purring, while I wheeled the case into the living room.

"You might need him," said Alissa. "Not that you can't defend yourself, Blair, but I can't help feeling that anyone who's been waiting for a chance to get at Rebecca has the opportunity now she's away from Fairy Falls."

"I know." Worry squirmed inside me. "Bu Madame Grey will be with us. Nathan too."

"Nathan?" she echoed and sipped her tea. "Why? Did he invite himself along to keep you company?"

"Mostly to spare me from having to make small talk with Blythe, I think."

She choked on her tea. "She's going as well? Really?"

"Why is everyone surprised?" I asked. "She's Rebecca's sister."

"She's also shown zero interest in her magic lessons so far or anything to do with her responsibilities as Head Witch."

"This is different from an exam, though." I thought back to her unusual level of concern when she'd met us at the coven's headquarters the previous day. "She seemed to think we'll need her help. Not sure why."

"The same reason I'm thinking of, I imagine," said Alissa. "She thinks that someone will try to make trouble at the meeting."

"Did your grandmother tell you that?" Madame Grey didn't usually discuss the council's current drama with her granddaughter, but it sounded like something she'd say.

"Not directly." She put her mug on the coffee table. "I just... please be careful, all right?"

"I will," I said. "Don't forget I'll have Sky and Nathan with me to help watch for trouble when the other witches are in the meeting." I wasn't sure whether I'd be let in, since

I wasn't a Head Witch or one of their assistants—not in an official capacity, anyway.

"I know." She got up and hugged me. "See you soon."

"Miaow." Sky walked out of the flat ahead of me while I checked I hadn't left anything behind before grabbing my suitcase handle again. *Here we go.*

We made a strange group when we left Fairy Falls together—Nathan and me, Madame Grey, Blythe, and Rebecca. Ahead walked our familiars, Sky and Toast, who pretty much ignored each other. *Nothing new there.* Sky was a loner, while other familiars were wary around him, knowing he wasn't the same as a regular cat. Both were equally devoted to protecting their owners, however, and I was glad to have their company.

We crested the hill, which overlooked the large expanse of the lake that bordered Fairy Falls on its right-hand side. A forest covered most of its edges, while endless fields and hills stretched beyond the horizon.

"Here will do." Madame Grey came to a decisive halt. "Wands out. Ready, Blair?"

"Erm... I think so." Since not all of us could fly, we'd opted to use transportation spells to travel to the meeting's location instead of using broomsticks.

Blythe pulled out her wand, while Rebecca lifted her sceptre.

I raised my wand and nodded to Nathan. "Ready?"

"Miaow," said Sky.

"Does that mean yes or no?" I held my wand firmly, willing my hand to stop shaking. "Ready?"

"I am," said Nathan. "Sky doesn't seem keen on the idea, though."

Sure enough, the little black cat turned away from us

and began to pad downhill, leaving our group behind. "Nice to know my familiar has faith in me."

Granted, he was quick on his feet and was also likely to spend the meeting roaming around outside. Yet his departure didn't help my nerves. If I got us lost in a random field, then I'd never live it down.

Nathan took my arm. "I have faith in you."

I gave him a smile and waved my wand. Nathan and I vanished from the field and reappeared on an empty hillside.

Nathan released my arm. "See?"

"We're here?" I looked around, seeing nothing but grassy fields and hills. Then I spotted the rest of our group standing on the hill opposite ours. At least I hadn't landed us in the middle of the lake.

Now for the tricky bit. The Knotgrass Coven, who'd won the right to hold this meeting, had built their headquarters in an isolated field surrounded by wards that made it impossible for anyone to enter except via the gates around the property. We'd have to go the rest of the way on foot.

Nathan and I joined Madame Grey and the others and walked across the hillside in a vague northwest direction. I could see several other witches crossing the nearby fields, too, and when a couple of blond witches swooped down on their broomsticks to land on the hillside, Rebecca's steps faltered.

"I have no idea who any of these people are," she whispered. "Is it too late for a do-over?"

"You'll be fine." Madame Grey swept into the lead, past the spot where the blond witches had landed.

Instead of making their way to the meeting, the pair appeared to be having a heated argument on the grass. One of them held a Head Witch's sceptre in her hand, and a red squirrel sat at her feet, its tail fluffed up. Her familiar, I guessed.

The second witch, who was older than the first by a fair bit, faced her with her hands on her hips. "You're being unreasonable, Robin."

"Mother, I appreciate the concern, but I am not being followed," said the witch with the sceptre. "We've wasted enough time on detours as it is, and we don't need to fly around the entire country just to prove a point."

"That's the kind of attitude that might get you killed," said the older witch. "Really, it's not too much of a stretch to assume that someone here might be—"

The younger woman cleared her throat. "Ah, we have company."

Dropping her argument smoothly, the older woman rotated in our direction. "I assume you're here for the meeting too. I am Lady Wildwood, leader of the Wildwood Coven. This is my daughter, Robin—"

"And Head Witch of our region," Robin interjected. "This is Tansy, my familiar."

The squirrel hopped onto her shoulder and squeaked a greeting while I pondered on why her mother was their local coven leader without being the Head Witch for their region. The younger witch must have claimed the sceptre instead. Interesting, though with the sceptre making the choice itself, it wasn't entirely unheard of.

"I am Madame Grey, leader of the Meadowsweet Coven of Fairy Falls."

"I'm Rebecca Dailey," said Rebecca in a clear, confident voice, as she'd practised. "I'm Head Witch for this region, and this is my familiar, Toast."

"I'm Blythe," said Blythe. "Rebecca's sister and mentor."

The latter was a stretch, though it sounded more impressive than implying she was here to babysit. Then I realised they expected me to introduce myself too.

"Ah, I'm Blair Wilkes. We... Rebecca and I are taking classes together." My face heated at the older Lady Wildwood's raised eyebrows, as if she couldn't fathom why a nobody like me had tagged along.

Luckily, Nathan came to my rescue. "I'm Nathan," he said smoothly. "I'm here as security, mainly. Shall we go?"

Grateful that he'd spared me any further embarrassment, I ducked my head as we resumed walking. Sky, I noticed belatedly, was nowhere in sight. I hoped he'd be on his way, because it couldn't be more obvious that I needed backup in social situations even more than in magical duels.

The older witch, Lady Wildwood, cast another distrustful look around before continuing downhill in front of her daughter. From what I'd heard of their argument, she knew more of the dangers of being Head Witch than Robin did, and I wondered if she'd expected to take the Head Witch title herself instead of it going to her daughter instead.

Robin fell into step with Rebecca. "Hey, Rebecca. I've heard a lot about you."

"Oh?" Rebecca asked. "What have you heard?"

"Only that you're the youngest Head Witch in a while," said Robin. "I was chosen unexpectedly too. This is my first meeting as well, but my grandmother said it's mostly an introductory one."

Rebecca began to relax a little the more Robin talked, while I found myself glad that she wasn't the only newcomer at the meeting. As for me, I took solace in the knowledge that at least Blythe was as out of place as I was, even if she was able to claim a family relationship with

Rebecca—never mind that I'd done far more to help in her magical training than Blythe had.

At least I had Nathan at my side. As we passed a small village tucked between two hills, he said in a low voice, "That's the nearest magical community."

"The coven can't be fond of their fellow paranormals, then." I spoke without thinking, but he inclined his head.

"You're not wrong there."

My heart skipped a beat. Evidently, he'd been here before, and if not during his time working security for Fairy Falls, it could only have been when he'd been a paranormal hunter.

Before I could ask any more questions, we came into view of a large manor house. High fences circled the vast grounds, preventing us from seeing much of the house itself. Statues of witches in flight decorated the chimneys and sloping roofs, while more stone carvings decorated the pillars that marked each section of the fence.

Wow. This is the place?

I stuck close behind Nathan as we approached the gates, through which we could see a number of other witches were already milling around inside the garden.

A voluptuous witch wearing a green velvet cloak met us outside. "Here for the meeting? I'm Arabella Knotgrass. This is my house."

Judging by the absence of a sceptre in her hand, I knew she wasn't a Head Witch, but her coven must be well-established to own a property of this size. The garden was already packed, and all eyes turned towards Rebecca when we entered. She'd been mentally prepared for the attention, but her shoulders tensed all the same. I didn't blame her. The garden was overwhelming enough on its own, a maze of sculptures and hedges circling fountains and vibrant flower beds. Yet even the scenery didn't overshadow the assembled Head Witches and coven leaders—the former easier to pick out because of their sceptres.

My gaze landed on a skinny red-haired girl, who couldn't be older than fourteen, clutching a vibrantly glowing sceptre. She didn't look that much older than Rebecca. Rebecca's gaze followed mine, her posture stiffening as it sank in that she wasn't the only minor who'd been chosen as a Head Witch.

Spotting us, the teenage witch glided over to our group and tilted her head to one side as she took in Rebecca's sceptre. "You must be Rebecca Dailey."

Rebecca's mouth parted. "I am, yes. You?"

"Didn't you read the list of attendees?" She gave a condescending laugh, which caused a flush to ignite in Rebecca's face. "I'm Coral Vervain, from the Vervain Coven."

"And I'm Robin Wildwood," said Robin, stepping in before the young witch could humiliate Rebecca any further. "From Wildwood Heath."

More introductions followed, but Coral Vervain continued to regard Rebecca as if she were a smudge of dirt on a pristine carpet. Annoyance prickled my shoulder blades, but nobody paid me any attention at all. It couldn't be clearer that non-Head Witches were little more than furniture, aside from Madame Grey and a few more coven heads who were respected in their own right. Blythe, Nathan, and I might as well have been invisible.

I scooted back to Nathan's side. "I didn't know there was another minor as Head Witch."

"With a terrible attitude," he said in an undertone.

"They shouldn't make kids into Head Witches," another nearby witch said in a carrying whisper. Tall and lean, she wore a brilliant white robe sparkling with purple stars that matched the light at the end of her sceptre. "They're too vulnerable. Easy targets for manipulation."

I might have asked what would make her say that, but at that moment, a brunette Head Witch approached *me* instead of the others. Holding her sceptre in one hand, she held out her other hand to shake mine.

"I'm Meredith Norwood. You're Blair Wilkes, right?"

"Yes." I shook her hand quickly, wondering if I was supposed to know who she was. Meredith wore a neat black cloak and a pair of silver earrings that jangled when she lowered her head.

"I just wanted to thank you in person," she said in a quiet voice. "For getting that Mrs Dailey jailed."

I blinked in surprise. "Erm... You're welcome."

"Yeah, she was a nasty piece of work. I always hoped someone would get her locked up."

I had to agree, but I'd been hoping to avoid the subject, especially with her two children nearby. As if following my line of thought, Meredith turned away from me and bounded over to Rebecca.

"You must be Rebecca," she said. "The youngest Head Witch. I bet your mother never saw that one coming."

Rebecca looked distinctly uncomfortable, but she managed a strained smile. "That's right. Nice to meet you."

"I'm Meredith Norwood, if you didn't hear," she added. "I think everyone's here, so they'll start the meeting soon."

"Yes, get on with it," said a sour-faced witch in her late forties with a nest of grey-brown hair. "No sense in waiting for the grass to grow."

I wondered who she was addressing an instant before the crowd fell silent, looking expectantly at the green-clad witch who'd let us into the garden. The gate closing behind her, Arabella Knotgrass clapped for attention.

"That's enough chit-chat," said Arabella. "Everyone into the meeting room. As per our rules, we have room for one assistant per Head Witch, no more."

The other witches entered the building through a pair of vast oak doors. Blythe stuck to Rebecca's side like glue, inviting herself into the meeting as her assistant. I wondered briefly if I should offer myself as Madame Grey's assistant, but she'd already gone into the hall ahead of the others, and I'd make myself look even more of a fool if I tried to barge in.

Instead, I waited with Nathan and tried to tell myself that I'd still be able to help Rebecca from outside. Okay, not many people had been left behind. Robin's familiar, Tansy, scurried up a nearby tree, but the garden was nearly empty.

Nathan gave me a searching look. "The witches' attitude isn't a reflection on you, Blair. Ignore them."

"I'm not qualified to be in there anyway," I said. "I just worry about her. Rebecca."

"I understand," said Nathan. "Blythe is there, though, and she's used to dealing with witches like those, I don't doubt."

"I imagine their mother probably gave them lessons." I grimaced. "Before Blythe left home."

I didn't blame her for moving out at the first opportunity. Her mother was horrible, and even Blythe at her worst hadn't been as bad as Mrs Dailey. Yet I couldn't help feeling a twinge of resentment towards her for snagging my place in the meeting.

"We haven't heard any movement from her direction," Nathan said. "Blythe's mother, that is. In case you were wondering."

"Are you getting regular reports, then?" I asked, surprised. "Or—I guess they'd go to Steve instead."

"I asked for him to pass on every report to me," Nathan said. "It's more my business than his, because I'm head of the security team, and several of my family members are still active hunters. Anyway, they keep me updated on the situation with Mrs Dailey. And the former Inquisitor too."

I shivered. Inquisitor Hare's real name was Rowe Clearwater. He was a fairy prince who'd disguised himself as a human and taken over the paranormal hunters in a quest for domination. I'd exposed him, but he'd escaped before we could arrest him and put him in the very prison he'd once presided over. As for where he'd gone, even my dad didn't know. According to him, the best-case scenario was that it'd take another few hundred years before he came back to bother anyone again. Fairies could afford to play the long game for much longer than the average person.

Nathan cleared his throat. "While they're inside, want to go and get coffee in the village? I know a place."

The offer was tempting, especially given how long the witches' meetings tended to go on for. "All right."

The nearby village had a cosy coffee shop in which Nathan and I sat talking for an hour then two. We might have stayed there all day if not for the ping on my phone that told me the meeting was over. Glad I'd told Rebecca to send me a text when she escaped, I rose to my feet.

"Bit of a long introduction," Nathan remarked. "Not that I'm surprised."

"Nor me." Witches were almost as good at talking one another's ears off as they were at casting spells, and I doubted Rebecca had been able to get a word in edgeways. "There'll probably only be a brief reprieve before the second meeting kicks off, but I can at least check she's okay."

The day was organised into hour-long meeting slots, according to Madame Grey. Since they'd already run overtime by an hour, it might end up going on long into the night at this rate. Nathan and I walked back to the house at a leisurely pace, which quickened when we saw that the garden was already full of cloaked witches.

Nathan and I entered the mazelike garden and were swept up in the crowd. I didn't see Rebecca among them, though I did spot Blythe awkwardly hovering near the stairs in front of the house, alone. It might be her status that had driven the other Head Witches to ignore her, but I had to wonder if it was partly because of her mother instead. Some of the other witches here might have been her supporters at one time, but after Mrs Dailey had been jailed, it'd be wise for them to keep that quiet.

"Where's Rebecca?" I whispered to Nathan.

That was when I heard the scream. *Rebecca.*

Adrenaline flooded me. I ran in the direction of the noise, ducking around hedges and flower beds. I had my wand in my hand before the second scream and skidded to a halt in a clearing.

There Rebecca stood, stunned, beside the limp body of Coral Vervain.

3

———

Rebecca met my eyes, her gaze filled with horror. Coral Vervain was unmistakeably dead, her limbs splayed at unnatural angles, as if she'd fallen from a great height. While Nathan caught up to me first, murmurs rose in the background as the other witches caught on to the disturbance.

"Murder!" someone shrieked, the shrill noise drawing more attention, and before long, we were surrounded.

It took me a while to spot Madame Grey among the others, and the hedges and fountains prevented her from getting any closer to the front of the crowd. A grey-haired Head Witch dressed in crimson robes, whom I'd heard the others call Jodie Atwater, elbowed her way to Coral Vervain's side.

"Her bones are broken," Jodie announced to the waiting witches. "Most likely by a breaking curse, cast using a sceptre. Make no mistake. Another Head Witch killed her."

All eyes turned to Rebecca, and my heart sank. Why had she been wandering around alone in the first place? A dozen questions swam in my mind, none of which I wanted to ask in front of an audience.

"You found her." Jodie Atwater addressed Rebecca. "Didn't you? Did you see who did this to her?"

"I didn't," said Rebecca. "I didn't see anyone else when I found her like this."

Several disbelieving whispers passed among the other witches. I should have expected them, but my hands curled into fists all the same.

"Why were you looking for her?" asked the witch I'd heard speak disparagingly of teenagers being chosen as Head Witches.

"Coral... she asked me to talk to her after the meeting," Rebecca mumbled. "I lost track of her when we left the house, but I thought I saw her walk past that hedge over there. Then I found her lying here."

"You didn't see her attacker?" asked Jodie Atwater in sceptical tones. "They disappeared into thin air, did they?"

Rebecca shook her head. "No. They must have come around the hedge from the other side."

My lie-sensing ability told me she spoke the truth, but the expressions on the other witches' faces suggested they believed otherwise. *Oh crap.* I was probably the only person here who could sense lies, and nobody else even knew I *had* that ability outside the small group who'd accompanied me from Fairy Falls. The other Head Witches might not even believe me, given that I had good reason to want to protect Rebecca.

"Is there a way to identify which sceptre was used to curse her?" I directed the question at Madame Grey. "You can identify whether a wand cast a particular spell, so can't we do the same with sceptres?"

"Sceptres are too volatile to test in that way," Madame

Grey replied. "That said, each sceptre can only be used by their current wielder, and that curse is a dangerous and little-known one."

"I doubt there's a Head Witch who doesn't know of the curse in theory, at least," said Jodie Atwater, who still had her eye on Rebecca. "Even the youngest among us."

"I swear I didn't," whispered Rebecca. "I didn't do anything to her. I don't know how to use that curse."

"As the overseer of Rebecca's training, I can verify that," added Madame Grey. "Coral Vervain was certainly killed by someone who wields a sceptre, but there's more than one of those present. Including Coral's own sceptre, which will need to be taken somewhere secure for the time being."

For a moment, all eyes turned towards where Coral's sceptre lay beside her crumpled body, its violet glow extinguished. Nobody volunteered to remove it.

"I think you're forgetting the important part," said Catherine Oakley, an elderly Head Witch who'd dressed in black, as if she was on her way to a funeral, not a meeting. "There's a killer hiding among us. We must call the police at once."

"We'll do no such thing," said Arabella Knotgrass. "My coven is the leading authority in this region, which means we have more authority than the police do."

"Certainly not," said Jodie Atwater. "The laws state that in cases like this—that is, a murder on the coven's property —then another impartial authority must be brought in."

"If all present Head Witches are potential suspects, then none of them counts as impartial," ventured Catherine Oakley. "As for the non-Head Witches, I see no reason not to simply nominate a coven leader to take on the questioning. If nobody else is willing, then I'll happily do it myself."

"Absolutely not," said Jodie Atwater. "Besides, the Head Witches aren't all equal suspects."

Everyone turned to Rebecca again.

"I think we could all use a refresher on the rulebook," said Madame Grey. "For a start, it's out of the question to entrust any Head Witch with the questioning. For another, finding the body is not an indicator of guilt, especially as we've established that Rebecca had no prior knowledge of the curse in question. Does anyone else have proof that they knew nothing of the curse? I'll wait."

Nobody spoke, and I felt a rush of gratitude towards Madame Grey for taking the attention off Rebecca *and* giving the Head Witches the choice between admitting to gaps in their knowledge or else potentially implicating their own involvement in a murder, neither of which would be great for their reputations. As for Blythe, she might at least have come to her sister's defence, given that she was the one who'd taken my spot in the meeting room. Why had she left her alone in the first place?

I wished Nathan and I had never left the property at all, but why had Rebecca gone off alone in the first place? Why would she want to meet with someone who'd treated her with such disdain? I'd have to ask her later, because the other witches showed no signs of leaving us to talk in peace. Not everyone looked convinced by Madame Grey's words either.

"There's one way to resolve this." Jodie Atwater lifted her sceptre and faced Rebecca, a gleam in her eye. "If we were to test each of the suspects on their self-defence skills, we might come up with some hidden knowledge they conveniently forgot they possessed."

What? She had to be joking. Luckily, before I could intervene, Arabella Knotgrass cleared her throat. "I would prefer it if you did not start a duel in my garden."

Jodie Atwater lowered her sceptre while I made a mental note to keep an eye on that one.

"As for the matter of finding the killer," Arabella Knotgrass added, "then any non-Head Witch ought to suffice as an impartial authority, shouldn't they? We know someone who wields a sceptre is responsible."

"Not necessarily," said Jodie Atwater. "If I wanted to assassinate someone and make it look like someone else was to blame, then the first thing I'd do was steal a sceptre."

"That's enough," said Madame Grey. "Lady Atwater, you know perfectly well that it isn't possible to steal *or* borrow another witch's sceptre. Besides, this isn't the time for speculation. Arabella Knotgrass, as you are the authority and owner of this house, I'd like you to assist me in moving the body to a more appropriate location."

"And the sceptre?" asked Catherine Oakley.

Madame Grey's gaze passed over our group, snagging on Nathan. "Nathan will carry the sceptre. As he's the only person among us who isn't a witch or a wizard, I think that's the best way forward, don't you?"

Nobody argued, for a wonder. They might not respect or trust Rebecca, but Madame Grey evidently had a reputation even among the Head Witches. At her command, everyone moved out of the clearing and into the main part of the garden, leaving a clear path for Madame Grey and Arabella Knotgrass to levitate Coral's body into the building. Nathan followed them, carrying the sceptre, while I waited next to Rebecca in case any of the other witches leapt on her and started flinging accusations again.

Soon, Madame Grey returned from the house. "As the leading witch of Rebecca's coven and the person responsible for her well-being, I would like to speak with her alone before anyone questions her."

"To give her a cover story, is that it?" Jodie Atwater scoffed.

"Certainly not." Madame Grey gave her a withering look that I wouldn't have wanted to be on the receiving end of. "Have I ever, in my decades of serving the community, given you any reason to doubt my intentions? Do you truly think I would intentionally stoop to protecting a murderer of a Head Witch? Rebecca is under my protection, and I wish to talk with her to find out her story of her discovery of Carol's murder. That is all."

Once again, her words had cowed everyone into silence, but while most of the witches present respected Madame Grey, they didn't trust Rebecca. I had no doubt the ones who disliked Mrs Dailey had already designated her as guilty, regardless of what her coven leader said in her defence.

"Now," said Madame Grey. "I'll talk to Rebecca myself first along with my companions from Fairy Falls. You're welcome to discuss contacting the police or otherwise deferring to another authority, which I believe is ultimately the decision of Arabella Knotgrass."

Arabella Knotgrass briefly looked startled to have Madame Grey's support after the others had shot down her ideas, but when the attention turned towards her, she smoothed out her expression. "Very well."

"That's not on," another Head Witch protested. "She can't make the decision for all of us at once. I say we should vote on how to proceed with the investigation."

"If you insist," said Madame Grey. "Before you vote, I'd advise you to consider your options carefully. Particularly the potential impact of bringing in an independent party."

What was the other option? Did she mean she wanted

one of us to take charge of the investigation instead? I couldn't see that going well either, if the job ended up being taken by someone who already thought Rebecca was guilty. I'd ask her once we were alone, so I climbed the stone stairs to the front of the building and joined Nathan and Blythe in the entrance hall.

Twice the size of the one inside our own coven's headquarters, the hall contained an array of potted plants, gilt-lined portraits that I assumed must show past coven leaders, and eye-wateringly bright gold wallpaper. Madame Grey led us into a vast meeting room dominated by a polished wooden table and with equally vibrant wallpaper. A crystal chandelier enhanced the effect even further.

"The Knotgrass Coven must have a massive budget," I remarked. "I feel like I should have worn sunglasses."

"They spend all their money on fancy spells to make their houses more interesting," Blythe said dismissively. "This is all an illusion. It's probably a dilapidated shack underneath."

I turned on her. "Why did you let your sister run off alone, Blythe?"

"I didn't *let* her." A flush crept across her cheeks. "I... I took a wrong turning on my way out of the meeting room and lost sight of her."

"You got lost." That was her excuse? "You were supposed to keep an eye on her at the bare minimum while I was stuck outside."

"I'm standing right here," Rebecca objected, her voice shaky. "It's my fault. Coral... she asked me to talk to her privately after the meeting and offered to give me tips on how to accelerate my magical skill with the sceptre. I was going to hear her out. That's all."

"So you went to talk to her alone?" I asked incredulously. "Without any of us?"

She dropped her gaze. "I'm a Head Witch. I can hardly bring my big sister or coven leader everywhere, and I didn't know someone was waiting to ambush her. By the time I found her, it was too late."

I didn't need a lie-sensing power to know she spoke the truth, but the other witches would be harder to convince. "Why'd she want to meet up alone?"

"Probably to lure you into a trap," said Blythe. "The same with her killer. They wanted to pin this on you, I bet."

She might be paranoid... or she might be right. "Who else knew you were meeting her?"

Rebecca shook her head. "We arranged it when we were leaving the meeting. Anyone might have overheard us."

"Including your sister?" I looked pointedly at Blythe. "I'm not saying you should have gone with her, but you should at least have been paying attention."

She flushed. "I was taking notes."

"It's done now," said Madame Grey. "And we'll have to work together if we're to stop the others from using this unfortunate death as a chance to discredit all of us at once. Is that clear?"

"Of course," I said. "I wonder, though... did the person who did this intend for Rebecca to take the blame? If they arrived here planning murder, I have trouble believing they knew Coral planned to meet her alone."

"Precisely," said Madame Grey. "There's a chance the person was targeting Coral Vervain alone, and Rebecca was a convenient scapegoat. No more."

"Who even *was* Coral Vervain?" I asked. "Aside from a prodigy, I mean."

Unlike Rebecca, she'd had extensive training as a Head Witch, but those skills hadn't saved her in the end.

"She was relatively new to the job," said Rebecca. "But like all Head Witches, she probably had enemies."

"Exactly," said Blythe. "I think the person who did this had something against both of you, but the rest of the witches want you arrested regardless of whether you committed the crime or not. That'd be far more convenient for the rest of them."

"Blythe," I said, though she might not be far wrong. "Not all of them will want to vote someone as guilty by committee, especially when Rebecca *doesn't* know how to use the curse that killed Coral Vervain. It's a safe bet all the others do, right?"

"Yes," said Madame Grey, "which means finding the actual killer will be tricky, especially given that they must have wanted this to be public. Personally, I think the other witches are most likely to opt for the committee method of questioning instead of nominating an individual. They'll pick out a panel of judges, essentially, to question all the suspects one at a time."

"I take it the panel won't consist of any of the other Head Witches," I said. "That still leaves quite a few people, yeah, but none of them is exactly qualified as an impartial judge. What's the alternative?"

"The police," said Nathan. "Or the local branch of hunters, who work closely with the police in question."

Ah. We don't want them *stepping in.* That would explain why Madame Grey had favoured putting the decision in the hands of one or more of the witches instead.

"I think some of the others will want the reassurance of the police's presence," said Madame Grey. "The problem is that the police weren't here at the time of the murder, and they don't understand all the covens' politics or the details of how the sceptres work. That Rebecca was found at the scene of the crime might be enough to condemn her."

Rebecca made a choked noise. "That's unfair."

"And dangerous," I said. "Considering the real killer is still here somewhere."

"If she's found guilty... she's a minor," Blythe intervened. "She can't be jailed, right?"

"Most likely, she'll be sent back to Fairy Falls for a trial if they do find her guilty," said Madame Grey.

"With our reputation in tatters," said Rebecca tremulously. "I can't let that happen, even if I don't end up jailed. What if the person who does the questioning is someone who hates us?"

"Then I'll see what I can do." Madame Grey looked between Rebecca and her sister. "My own reputation will shield you from the others' anger to some degree, but I won't be able to take part in the questioning myself, because of my connection to you."

"Then who?" I asked. "Nobody here isn't biased in some way. Even those of us who can sense truth from lie."

Even Nathan, though he wasn't a witch, was biased by virtue of his relationship with me. As for me, I might have my lie-sensing power, but that didn't give me a position of authority.

Madame Grey's attention focused on me. "I can mention your ability to the others, with your permission, but I doubt they'll agree to let you take over the questioning, because of your connection with Rebecca. If I were in your place, I might use your talents in a subtler way. Also, I don't doubt that many of the witches present at the meeting are used to evading lies, and the killer may even have taken your talents into account when they planned this."

"They might have already known about my ability?" I hadn't even thought of that possibility, but given the publicity around my clash with the hunters, it wouldn't surprise me if word had reached at least some of our fellow Head Witches. "It's worth trying, though, isn't it?"

"Yes." She drew in a breath. "I will talk with the others and see what they have decided."

Madame Grey left the room while I waited with Blythe and Rebecca. It seemed impossible that a room this big could even fit inside the building, and I might have believed it to be the result of a fairy illusion, if I didn't know better. This was all a witch's handiwork—or several of them.

Blythe and I studiously ignored each other for a few minutes before Madame Grey returned to the room.

"The witches weren't able to agree on one person to do the questioning," she said. "Or bringing in the police."

"Then what are they going to do?" I asked. "The committee approach?"

"Correct," she said. "Their compromise is to let anyone who isn't a suspect sit on a committee while all the suspects are questioned one at a time."

"Then the committee votes on whether they're guilty or not?" asked Blythe. "They can't vote my sister as a killer."

"It's the Head Witches who are more likely to believe she's guilty, and none of them will be on the committee," said Madame Grey. "Unfortunately, neither will any of us."

"We'll be allowed into the meeting, though, won't we?" I asked.

"If I have my way, yes," she said. "If necessary, I'll insist on you and Blythe being present, Blair. You're witnesses, after all, and as for your ability... you can decide whether or not to be open about it."

"If I am, they might decide I'm still biased in favour of

my own coven," I said. "But if someone gives the game away when they're being questioned, and my lie-sensing power catches them out, then it's got to count for something."

Were things ever that simple? In my experience, they weren't, but one never knew.

"Nathan, you can decide for yourself whether to come to the meeting," Madame Grey said. "You might want to give Steve a call."

"Do you want *him* sticking his nose in?" I queried.

"I'm actually required to tell him if anything like this happens," Nathan said apologetically. "I hoped I wouldn't have to, but it's the rules."

"Then the whole of Fairy Falls is going to know by the day's end."

"That was inevitable no matter what," said Madame Grey. "Steve won't volunteer to come here himself, even if the witches are unable to come to a definite conclusion."

"What, then?" I asked. "What if they disagree or otherwise can't get a certain answer on who's guilty?"

"That, I don't know," she said. "In the meantime, however, there are certain people among us who are capable of gathering evidence that nobody else will pick up on."

She looked at me then at Blythe, and the penny dropped. "You mean you want me and Blythe to investigate ourselves. Right?"

"Correct," she said. "I have a feeling this murder is more complicated than it appears from the outside, and it's possible one questioning won't be enough. I'll do what I can to unearth the truth, but I'm in a conspicuous position."

She had a point. Blythe didn't look thrilled at the idea of working with me, but I was willing to do anything to help Rebecca, even join forces with my former co-worker. Her ability to read minds combined with my lie-sensing power ought to get us somewhere, though it didn't mean we'd necessarily find out who was to blame.

And whether we'd be able to accuse anyone without the other witches objecting on the grounds of our being biased in Rebecca's favour remained to be seen.

I inclined my head. "Okay. I'll sit in on the questioning and see if anyone drops any obvious lies. Blythe... you can sense their thoughts, right?"

"Do you think I can read the minds of witches as skilled as they are?" she scoffed. "Some, yes, but the killer will probably have prepared for that possibility too."

Typical. "It's worth a try."

"Good." Madame Grey made for the door again. "The others will be conducting their questioning in here, so I'll let them know the room is free, and I'll be back shortly."

When she'd gone, Blythe glared at me. "Great. Just what I need when my sister's freedom is on the line. Having to depend on your unreliable talents."

"I'm not that happy either, you know." Did she have to pick *now* to start griping at me? "Why did you let the other Head Witches accuse your sister of murder?"

"What was I supposed to do? Start a fight with a dozen Head Witches at once?"

"You might have come to her defence," I said. "Or spoken a word in her favour."

"She's already being judged," she said. "I wouldn't do anything but make myself look biased."

"You're supposed to be biased. You're her *sister*."

"Drop it." Rebecca's weary tone sounded far older than her age, which wasn't a surprise with everything else she had to shoulder, and a fresh wave of determination seized me in its grip. She didn't deserve this, not after the hell her mother had put her through already.

"It's not done," I said to Blythe. "Not until we find the real killer's identity and expose them."

"It won't be as easy as all that," she said. "This was planned."

"I thought that was why you came. To stop this kind of thing." At a warning look from Rebecca, I dropped the subject.

The door opened soon after, and Madame Grey entered, followed by a line of other witches. With comparatively little fuss, they split into two groups. The Head Witches sat at one side of the table, and everyone else claimed the other, while Blythe and I hovered awkwardly in between, not part of either.

Madame Grey pulled out a chair at the very end of the table and beckoned Blythe and me to join her. Presumably, this was the designated area for those of us who were considered too biased to make a judgement.

As we looked upon the Head Witches sitting at the table, a chill ran down my spine at the sight of Coral Vervain's empty seat.

Someone in this room was a murderer... and I might be the only person who could find them.

4

With everyone sitting in the meeting room, the questioning kicked off. The other witches had apparently decided there was no need to repeat their introductions, leaving me to guess the identities of the ones I hadn't already spoken to—of both the Head Witches and the committee who might decide Rebecca's fate.

"Let's begin," said Arabella Knotgrass, who seemed to have appointed herself the leader of the questioning despite the others' earlier objections. "We've decided to approach this in a fair manner, so each Head Witch will give their story of what they were doing at the time of Coral Vervain's death and explain their relationship to the victim. At the end, we'll evaluate the evidence and make a decision. Does anyone have an objection?"

A few mutters arose among the witches, but nobody spoke up.

In the ensuing quiet, I leaned over to Blythe and whispered, "You're going to have to tell me who these people are, you know. I'm not going to be any help if you don't."

Part of me expected her to refuse out of sheer stubbornness, but she gave a reluctant nod. "Fine, but it's not my problem if you forget."

"To start off with," said Arabella Knotgrass, "I'd like to invite Rebecca Dailey to give her account of the events surrounding Coral Vervain's murder."

Rebecca repeated her story from earlier. Every word was true, of course, and I didn't need a lie-sensing power to know that.

"You claim not to have known the victim before today?" asked Arabella.

"I didn't," said Rebecca. "I didn't even know there was another Head Witch who was underage until we met."

"Did you feel she might be a threat to you?"

"Not at all," said Rebecca. "In fact, she offered to give me some tips. That's why I was going to meet with her."

True.

"I think that's clear enough," Madame Grey said. "For my part, I was unaware of Coral Vervain's age before we arrived here, though I knew her name. That's all I passed on to Rebecca."

"Yes, you're her... mentor? Or teacher?" Arabella raised a brow while mutters sprang up around her.

"Her coven leader," said Madame Grey. "I did give her private lessons to fill in the gaps in her knowledge of the Head Witches and the regional covens, since the former Head Witch for our region declined to play a part in passing on lessons to her successor."

Did she now? It didn't surprise me. Aveline Hollyhock had not wanted to be replaced, least of all by an eleven-year-old.

"Did she perhaps object to the new Head Witch's family members?" Jodie Atwater ventured. "Some might consider it unwise for the region to have selected a Head Witch with family ties to someone who tried to overthrow the council."

More whispers sprang up, and I suppressed the urge to tell her Aveline Hollyhock had absolutely nothing to do with the issue at hand. I should have known someone would bring up Rebecca's mother sooner or later, though.

Madame Grey cleared her throat. "Might I remind you that another member of Rebecca's family is present?"

The others looked at Blythe and me as if they'd forgotten we existed. I wished I could be as calm in a crisis as Madame Grey was, disdainful as she addressed the table at large.

"Furthermore," said Madame Grey, "I believe we're here to discuss the circumstances of Coral Vervain's death and the potential involvement of each Head Witch in the room, *not* dissect the family of one particular Head Witch. If there is reason to return to the subject later, then do so, but don't forget the purpose of our meeting."

More mutters travelled up and down the table.

Catherine Oakley spoke first. "Yes, we are here to question all the present Head Witches, not just Rebecca. I vote we move on."

"I have one question first," said Jodie Atwater. "Why is Rebecca's sister present? Along with... who's the other one?"

Heat rushed to my face when the faintest smirk crossed Blythe's face for an instant, but I straightened upright in my seat. "I'm Blair Wilkes. Rebecca and I knew each other before she became Head Witch. I've helped her in her training."

"I invited Blair to attend the meeting," said Madame Grey. "Since she wasn't in the grounds of the house at the time of Coral Vervain's death, she's an objective outsider."

"Objective?" asked Jodie Atwater. "She's friends with the suspect."

At the sight of the open condescension on the others' faces, I'd had enough. "As a matter of fact, I'm here because I have the ability to sense truth from lie. I've used it to help out in investigations before, so if anyone in this room lies, I'll instantly know."

A ripple of interest passed among the others, but not everyone looked surprised at my revelation. That much, I'd expected, though it didn't mean they'd take my abilities seriously.

"You came here with Rebecca Dailey," said Arabella Knotgrass. "For what reason? Did you think you'd need to make use of your talents before you reached here?"

"I hoped I wouldn't."

Amid the others' whispers, I distinctly heard the name "Mrs Dailey." It was no secret that I'd played a major role in exposing her, and perhaps it was time to stop tiptoeing around the subject. "I came here because I've been supporting Rebecca since before she was chosen as Head Witch. I didn't expect to end up in that position, but I felt obligated to help her. After all, my abilities helped see to her mother's arrest for treason."

"Correct." Madame Grey cut through the others' whispers. "Blair is the reason Mrs Dailey is currently behind bars, and this is the last time we'll mention her by name."

Blythe shifted in her seat. "Agreed. Also, I should mention to all of you that I can read minds."

What was that for? Had she assumed my admission of my lie-sensing ability was a challenge to her own standing here, however precarious it might be?

"Can you, now?" Unimpressed, Jodie addressed the room at large. "Maybe this one should sit with the suspects.

Can we trust someone with a family history such as hers? She might have wanted Coral Vervain out of the picture from the start."

"Of course I didn't," Blythe said. "I didn't know Coral existed until today."

Lie.

I dropped my gaze, trying to mask my surprise. Blythe was lying? If she'd known about Coral Vervain—even her age—I could understand why she hadn't told Rebecca, but I hadn't realised that my lie-sensing power might backfire on my allies.

"And your mother?" Arabella Knotgrass ventured. "She didn't send you here?"

"No," said Blythe. "Absolutely not. I don't support my mother, and besides, she's in jail. I never want to see her again."

That, at least, was true. "She's telling the truth."

Jodie scoffed. "You're her friend, so of course you'd come to her defence."

"No, we're not friends," Blythe and I said at more or less the exact same time.

"But we both hate Mrs Dailey as much as Rebecca does," I added. "I have absolutely no idea what Mrs Dailey would possibly have had to gain from having Coral Vervain killed. Assuming she had a hand in it at all, which I doubt, since she's locked in a high-security prison."

"That is enough," said Madame Grey. "I told you, Lady Atwater, we're not here to discuss Mrs Dailey or her transgressions. Who wants to be questioned next?"

Given the way Jodie Atwater and the witch next to her were muttering to each other, I knew they certainly weren't finished with the subject, but I tuned them out. I was lucky they'd let me into the room at all, and I had more important things to concern myself with than their pettiness, like listening for possible lies.

Speaking of which, I'd have to wait until after the meeting to ask Blythe why she'd lied about not knowing Coral Vervain had existed before the meeting. Maybe she'd wanted to shield her sister from the knowledge that there was another young Head Witch out there who was more accomplished than she was. Had Blythe forgotten about my ability, or had she trusted me not to call her out? As far as lies went, it wasn't a serious one, but she'd put me in an awkward position.

Trying to put it out of mind, I focused my full attention on the questioning and tried to pick out any lies. That wasn't easy, because everyone had a similar story of what had happened after the meeting, which left plenty of room for omissions. I also took it as a given that everyone except Rebecca knew how to use the deadly curse that had killed Coral, which didn't help me narrow it down any further.

That left me with little choice but to zero in on anyone who had a prior connection with Coral and a possible reason to murder her. The witch talking to Jodie Atwater— who Blythe whispered to me was called Brenna Thorngrove —was one I had a particular eye on, because she'd spoken with disdain about both Rebecca *and* Coral Vervain. When it came to her turn, Brenna Thorngrove gave her story of the day's events, like the others, and then we moved on to her actual thoughts on the victim and the suspect.

"I don't think she should have been Head Witch," said Brenna Thorngrove. "I made no secret of that. That doesn't mean I wished her harm."

She spoke the truth, as far as I could tell.

"And Rebecca?" I asked her, unable to help myself. "Did you wish *her* harm?"

"Absolutely not," she said. "I simply wished there was a way for her to resign her position without breaking with tradition."

True. Her words kicked off an argument among the others concerning the actual Head Witch regulations. I'd already asked Madame Grey if the rules contained a clause for a Head Witch to resign if they were underage, and she'd said no, the sceptre's word was considered law. When the argument petered out, we moved to the next suspect: Robin Wildwood. She gave her story, which contained no lies.

"I knew of Rebecca," she said. "That is—I knew a child had recently been chosen as Head Witch shortly before I was picked myself. I knew about Coral being a minor, too, but I didn't know she existed until a few days ago."

True.

"Anything else?" asked Arabella.

"Yes. Tansy told me that she saw Coral leave the gathering alone, from where she was watching from up a tree," said Robin. "She didn't see who attacked her, but she believes that someone was waiting to ambush her in the garden."

Tansy? Oh, she meant her squirrel familiar. Could she *talk* to her familiar? It sounded like it. I hadn't known it was possible for familiars to communicate in words. In any case, my lie-sensing ability informed me that she'd told the truth.

The last witch to be questioned was Meredith Norwood, one of the handful of people in the room who'd both been kind to Rebecca and who'd thanked me for seeing to Mrs Dailey's imprisonment.

"I don't believe Mrs Dailey was involved in this," Meredith told the other witches. "Her daughters definitely weren't, anyway. They want nothing to do with her."

True... but her own words carried a speculative note that

made my lie-sensing power unable to come away with a definite answer. She didn't *believe* Mrs Dailey was involved, but that didn't mean it was true. It wouldn't have surprised me if Rebecca's mother had wanted to disrupt the meeting, but I'd thought her allies were thoroughly cowed by her arrest and imprisonment.

Regardless, we'd reached the end of the questioning. The room's attention returned to the committee, who'd have to make a decision on whether anyone had demonstrated enough guilt to be questioned further.

"Before that," said Madame Grey, "I wanted to ask if Blair has anything she wants to share with us."

I shook my head. "No. Ah, nobody told a lie that implicates them in guilt of the murder of Coral Vervain. That said, Rebecca also told the truth. She isn't the killer."

"Then what do you propose we do? Use the process of elimination?" asked Catherine Oakley.

"Why are we depending on the abilities of someone with a connection to the main suspect?" Jodie Atwater queried. "Let us vote to determine Rebecca Dailey's guilt, and that'll be that."

My heart lurched. "You can't vote on whether she's guilty or not. A vote won't change the truth."

"A vote is all we have," Arabella Knotgrass said. "So, who thinks Rebecca is guilty?"

A few hands among the council went up but not the majority. Relief swept over me followed by alarm when Jodie Atwater got to her feet with her sceptre in both hands. "This is absurd. It's no way to solve a crime."

"Would you have said the same if they'd voted her guilty?" I cut off in a gasp when Blythe elbowed me hard in the ribs.

"What do you suggest instead?" Catherine Oakley asked

of Jodie Atwater. "We already voted against bringing in outsiders, though maybe some of us have since changed their minds."

As more protests arose, Madame Grey leaned over to me and whispered, "I'll calm them down. Can you find Nathan and ask if he's heard from Steve yet?"

"Sure." All too happy to leave the witches to their bickering, I made my way to the door.

To my consternation, Blythe came with me. I might have reprimanded her for leaving her sister again, but Madame Grey was sitting right next to Rebecca, and once we were outside the room, I finally had the chance to talk to Blythe alone.

I rubbed my sore ribs, narrowing my eyes at her. "I know you weren't telling the truth when you said you didn't know Coral Vervain existed before the meeting."

"Your point?"

"I just wondered why. I understand why you didn't want Rebecca to know, but I didn't expect my lie-sensing power to react to you."

"I don't know why you're surprised. Not everyone is perfectly honest."

"It's not the lie that's the problem," I said. "If you're keeping something from me and your sister that might help us to prove her innocence, I'd appreciate it if you could tell me."

"I'm not."

"Then why lie?"

"Because," she said through gritted teeth, "I've heard that our delightful mother has recently been receiving visitors to her jail cell and that Coral Vervain might have been one of them."

My throat went dry. "Who told you that?"

"It doesn't matter."

"It certainly does. Did you tell Madame Grey?"

Her silence said it all. I suppressed a groan. "Blythe, I don't want your sister getting arrested, but this is the kind of detail that needs to be shared if we're to prove she's innocent. You can tell *me* how you found out. You're not still in touch with your mother, are you?"

"No," she muttered. "Never."

"Nathan's supposed to get regular updates from the hunters assigned to watch her," I said. "I'll see if *he's* heard anything."

"Feel free." She turned away. "But please don't tell my sister."

"What?" She had to be joking. "I'm not keeping something like that a secret from her, Blythe."

"You're the only one who can lie without at least one person in the room instantly knowing," she said. "Besides, does she really need to be burdened by that knowledge?"

"If it links to Coral's death?" I asked. "Yes, especially if someone wanted to frame her for murder. Do you have any intention of telling Madame Grey at all? Because even if I don't tell your sister, I'll certainly tell *her*."

"I thought you'd say that." She veered towards the meeting room again. "You know, I dipped into a few people's thoughts during the meeting. They're not all as adept at shielding as you are, and I think some of them are holding back information."

"What does that mean?" I stared blankly after her. "Blythe, it's not a contest. This is your sister's safety we're talking about."

She didn't turn back, so I sighed and then went looking for Nathan. One would've thought he would have heard if there'd been any activity involving Mrs Dailey, given that he'd been watching the scenario from Fairy Falls, but he hadn't mentioned anything to me. How could Blythe be aware and not the town's security team? Let alone Madame Grey?

It took me several minutes to find my way across the lobby to the front door. I could have sworn it wasn't in the same place it'd been before, though the mirrors interspersed with the doors to classrooms made it tricky to tell which side of the hall I was on. Then once I got outside, I had to circle the house from behind before I found Nathan near a patch of hedges, his phone in his hand.

"There you are," I said. "I... what's going on?"

Nathan's face was ashen. "Sorry, Blair. The hunters have refused point-blank to let the witches handle this investigation themselves. They're sending someone here at once to take over the questioning until the killer is found."

5

I stared at Nathan, my heart sinking. The hunters were coming *here*? Did they intend to take over the trial altogether? "When are they coming?"

"Soon," he said. "They're walking here from the nearest branch, which is less than half an hour away."

"Oh no." In my experience, the hunters delighted in nothing more than interrogating people, and to have the opportunity to put a whole roomful of Head Witches on trial must have felt like Christmas had come early. And they'd have an excuse to discredit the regional witch councils *and* the Head Witches in the process.

"Exactly," he said. "When I called Steve, he insisted on putting me directly in contact with the local police, and the next thing I knew, the hunters had leapt on the call to demand they should be allowed to get involved. According to them, every person in that council room is too biased to be able to judge anyone's guilt."

"But the hunters are predisposed to be biased against the covens in general," I pointed out. "And... what about Rebecca? Are they likely to believe her guilty or not?"

"That, I don't know," said Nathan. "Once they hear she was the one who found the body, they'll certainly want to question her."

"She doesn't even know how to use the curse that killed the victim," I protested. "Won't they take that into account?"

"Yes, but that doesn't preclude her involvement," he said. "According to them, anyway."

"The others have already grilled her intensively." But that wouldn't make a difference to the hunters. "If the hunters hated her mother, then they'll already be inclined to see her as the villain. Even if they *didn't* hate Mrs Dailey, then it might not go well for her either, since Rebecca has never been on her mother's side."

I couldn't even begin to think of the potential consequences if the hunters who came here turned out to be Mrs Dailey's supporters—former or current. In fact, it might even be more dangerous for Rebecca than the alternative.

"I'm afraid I have no idea of the allegiances of the specific hunters they're sending," he said. "If they *do* believe her mother might be involved, then they're more likely to blame anyone who has a history of allying with Mrs Dailey, which doesn't include Rebecca, as a minor who was held against her will."

"Would they take that into account, though? They lived under the same roof for years." I lowered my gaze. "Besides, nobody is going to willingly admit to having been an ally to a criminal who was jailed for treason."

"Of course not," he said. "That doesn't mean it's impossible to find out, though."

"But..." I hesitated. "Did you hear that Mrs Dailey has apparently been having visitors? According to Blythe, anyway."

"Where'd she hear that?" he asked. "I certainly haven't

heard of anything from the direction of the jail. Like I told you, she's been quiet."

"She didn't tell me how she knew," I said. "I think Blythe has got it into her head that we're competing against each other in some way, so she's being even more tight-lipped than usual. Perhaps she knows someone who works at the prison."

"She might." His expression turned preoccupied. "My own connections are tenuous because I'm not an active hunter, and my family aren't best pleased with me after my actions in the past year. It's possible some information has passed me by."

How could Blythe be aware and not Nathan, though? "She mentioned Coral Vervain having met with her mother at some point, so the hunters might want to look into that one."

"I'll mention it to them," he said. "Though it wouldn't surprise me if they withheld information because they don't see me as trustworthy anymore."

"That's unfair," I said. "Not to mention dangerous for everyone you're trying to protect by keeping in contact. What did Steve have to say, anyway?"

"He told me to leave him out of it."

"Figures." That might be for the best, though. Steve wasn't exactly the kind of guy one wanted to have around in a crisis, and he wasn't a fan of me *or* Rebecca. "I guess someone has to break the bad news to the others."

Meaning me. I wouldn't subject Nathan to that task, not when he already had to deal with the hunters.

"I take it the witches weren't able to come to a definite decision on anyone's guilt?" he queried.

"No, they weren't," I said. "None of them told any obvious lies, but I had to expose my lie-sensing power to be allowed to stay in the room, so it's possible they figured out how to get around it. Blythe used her mind-reading powers, but she told me that a lot of Head Witches can shield against that kind of thing and that some of them were keeping secrets she couldn't detect. The only person with an actual useful update was Robin's squirrel familiar, who was sitting up in a tree at the time of the murder."

"Good to know," said Nathan. "I wish I had time to check in with the prison guards about Mrs Dailey, but the hunters will be here within the hour, and I'll have to welcome them myself."

"Fun." I really didn't want to be the person to tell the Head Witches that their authority was about to be usurped, but I had little choice in the matter. "Good luck. I'm going back into the trenches."

Hoping Madame Grey had managed to stop their argument at the very least, I returned to the entrance hall—and then stared in confusion. The golden wallpaper and portraits had vanished, to be replaced by towering mirrors that covered every inch of the walls. The doors seemed to have shifted around, too, and it took me several minutes to track down Blythe outside the meeting room.

"What's happened in here?"

"This whole house is covered with an automatic redecoration charm," Blythe said through pursed lips. "I thought you'd have recognised it from work."

"From..." *Oh.* My boss, Veronica, must have a similar spell on her office. It was the first time in a long while that Blythe had alluded to the fact that we'd once been co-workers, but that wasn't the important issue at hand. "We have a problem. Nathan told me the hunters are coming to take over the investigation, whether any of us likes it or not. Do you want to tell the others, or should I?"

Blythe swore, and I hastened to enter the meeting room before she found a way to blame me for it. While the décor in the room had changed to match the entrance hall, at least it appeared that nobody had started duelling with their sceptres in my absence. As the council members were still engaged in arguments and discussions, I made my way around the table without anyone acknowledging me and then whispered the unwelcome news to Madame Grey.

"I thought they would," she murmured. "I'll tell them."

"Thanks," I breathed, relieved that I wouldn't have to give the council yet another reason to distrust me.

Raising her voice, Madame Grey addressed the table. "I'm afraid several members of the local branch of the paranormal hunters are on their way here to take over the investigation."

"They what?" Arabella Knotgrass stared at Madame Grey before wheeling on her fellow Head Witches. "This is your doing, Catherine Oakley."

"Don't be absurd," Catherine replied. "You didn't think they'd take an interest the instant they heard one of us was murdered?"

"You've wanted them to be involved from the start. Don't deny it," Arabella said shrilly. "I will *not* have them invading my coven's home."

Accusations flew back and forth across the table, but Rebecca didn't say a word. The colour had drained from her face, but with the other Head Witches in my way, I couldn't get close enough to offer her any reassurance.

"Enough!" Madame Grey said finally. "Is this really the impression we want to give to the paranormal hunters? Do we want them to believe we can't get through a single meeting without breaking into an unproductive argument?"

That wasn't untrue, but the hunters didn't need any

more ammunition to use against us. The fact that one Head Witch had died at the hands of another was bad enough on its own.

"The hunters have an agenda," said the sour-faced witch who sat among the coven leaders. "They want us to disband."

"That might be true, but we don't need to give them a reason to undermine us," said Madame Grey.

"Then arrest her." Jodie Atwater pointed at Rebecca. "She's the obvious culprit, and if they see that we've already found the killer, there's no need for them to intervene."

"Do you really think they'll take your word for it?" Meredith Norwood enquired. "They don't trust our judgement either way, so there's no sense in trying to condemn an innocent person just to make them go away."

"Innocent?" Jodie Atwater scoffed. "As innocent as her mother, I'm sure. I wonder if the hunters remember Mrs Dailey. In fact, what if they turn out to be her allies?"

I'd wondered the same myself, but her words kicked off another argument among the witches. Nobody was going to admit to ever having been an ally of Mrs Dailey's, but what if the hunters *were* her former supporters? What would that mean for Rebecca?

"That's enough speculation," said Brenna Thorngrove. "Like it or not, the hunters are taking over the investigation, which means we have to let them. It's the quickest way to get this done."

"In my own house? I don't think so." Arabella Knotgrass scowled.

"They're already coming," Madame Grey said. "They know the facts about Coral Vervain's death and the discovery of her body. I believe they'll want to talk to everyone individually."

"Like any police investigation," added Catherine Oakley. "They'll be impartial."

"Aside from the fact that they want us shut down," added the sour-faced witch who'd commented earlier.

When I gave Blythe a questioning look, she begrudgingly whispered to me that the witch's name was Stephanie Underhill.

"That's a good-enough reason to play by the rules," said Brenna Thorngrove, cutting through the others' protests. "No scapegoating anyone, no starting unnecessary arguments, and no trying to undercut our visitors. We want the killer brought to justice, and so do they. We'll give them no reason to make trouble for us, and they won't. It's that simple."

"As if they haven't been waiting for this chance for months, if not years," Stephanie Underhill muttered. "They'll want trouble whether we give it to them or not."

Apparently, she had no intention of letting the subject drop, but I was inclined to agree with Brenna. The best course of action was to find the killer and to give the hunters no reason to interfere more than they were already inclined to—just as long as they didn't automatically assume Rebecca was guilty the way some of the witches had.

The problem was that everyone in the room had their own agendas, not just the hunters. Either they disliked Rebecca and wanted her jailed, or they wanted the hunters to step in for their own reasons, or they wanted the hunters to stay out of the investigation, no matter what the consequences were for the rest of us. If we weren't careful, it was Rebecca who'd end up taking the fall, no matter the outcome.

The arguments petered out when the door opened

again, and Nathan entered the room. "The hunters are here."

"Already?" whispered one of the witches. "I bet they were waiting outside the doors for something to go wrong."

As more mutters broke out along the table, Madame Grey cleared her throat. "I would advise everyone to think very carefully about the impression they want to give to the hunters, both of the Head Witches as a whole and of their own covens. *Everyone.* Is that clear?"

Silence filtered through the room as her words sank in. Within a minute, footsteps sounded outside the door, which creaked inward as several newcomers entered the meeting room. I counted six hunters, all of whom were male, save for one severe-looking dark-haired woman. All were under-dressed compared to the witches, clad in their usual plain trousers and jackets, which looked more like they were going hiking than heading a police investigation.

"I am Linda Graham," said the female hunter, displaying no fear at addressing some of the most powerful witches in the country. "I'm here to head this investigation on behalf of the authorities of Knotgrass Hill as well as the paranormal hunters as a collective. For the purposes of this investiga-tion, I would like to request that everyone stay on the prop-erty, if not inside this room, while we conduct the questioning."

"Everyone?" One of the coven leaders pointed at the row of Head Witches on the opposite side of the table. "Those are the suspects. The murderer used a sceptre to curse the victim, and sceptres can only be used by their owners. There's no need to place restrictions on those of us who don't have access to the murder weapons, is there?"

"As a matter of fact, there is," she said. "Not least because it would be unprofessional for us to make assumptions based on who you believe the suspects to be rather than our own observations. Our questioning will cover *everyone*, not just those who wield sceptres. To start off with, who accompanied the victim to the meeting?"

A ripple of surprise travelled among the witches, who'd presumably been expecting Rebecca to be questioned first, but nobody raised an objection.

"I did," said a dark-skinned witch who sat among the coven leaders and other non-Head Witches. "But I'm not—I can't use a sceptre."

Linda Graham ignored her protest. "Who else was acquainted with the victim prior to attending the meeting?"

The other witches were plainly displeased at this turn of events, but it was entirely possible that the murderer had had accomplices among the non-Head Witches, and the only way to root them out was to question everyone. At Linda's command, three witches followed her from the room to be questioned alone, while two of the hunters stayed in the meeting room, presumably to make sure nobody else wandered off.

"We're expected to sit in here all day?" Stephanie Underhill objected. "What if the questioning takes hours?"

"You can leave the room, as long as you stay on the property," said the nearest hunter, a heavyset man with his hair buzzed short. "Who is in charge of hosting this meeting?"

"I am," Arabella Knotgrass said. "I would prefer for my guests not to feel as if I am keeping them trapped inside my house."

I saw her point. While letting everyone leave would risk the killer vanishing inside the house's perplexing dimensions, I couldn't say I was keen on the idea of spending all day stuck in a room full of angry witches while they were questioned one at a time. More to the point, this might be my last chance to talk to Rebecca alone before her questioning.

"Then by all means, leave," said the hunter.

While some of the witches left the room, I crossed the table to Rebecca's side. "Want to go and get some air?"

"I'll be questioned soon," she whispered. "I can guarantee someone will tell them I found the body."

"At least you'd get it over with," I murmured back, conscious of the other witches watching us—and the hunters too. "It seems fairer than the alternative."

Rebecca wore a sceptical expression, but she begrudgingly followed me out of the room. Madame Grey, notably, remained behind, her gaze fixed on the hunters guarding the doors.

"I wonder if they'll want to question her as well," I whispered to Rebecca. "I guess I'm in the clear, since I wasn't actually on the property at the time... though they might single me out because of my connection with you."

Rebecca said nothing. I glanced at her and saw her gaze was downcast, her sceptre clutched in both hands.

"It'll be okay," I told her. "The real culprit won't be able to hide forever."

"I thought this meeting would just be about proving I'm worthy of the sceptre," she mumbled. "Not fighting for my freedom."

"The others weren't prepared for this either," I reminded her. "Certainly not for the hunters' involvement."

"That Catherine Oakley wanted them here," she said. "I wonder if she called them herself, in fact."

"I don't think she did, but you're right." I thought back. "She did seem overly keen to let them step in. I wonder why."

Blythe stepped out from behind a nearby potted plant. "It wasn't Catherine. She's not the killer."

"How do you know that?" If Blythe had a definite idea about the potential guilt of the others, it would have been nice if she'd told me sooner.

"She might want the hunters here, but she's not the sort to commit murder on a whim," Blythe answered. "She's served as a Head Witch almost as long as Aveline Hollyhock did."

True. "Anything else you haven't told me that might be useful?"

She glared at me in response, while Rebecca frowned in puzzlement. I didn't want to mention Blythe neglecting to tell me that Mrs Dailey had been having visitors when she'd clearly decided she didn't want Rebecca to know, but I *had* intended to tell Madame Grey. Though that would have to wait until after she was out of sight of the hunters.

I peered into the meeting room to see Madame Grey talking to the hunters beside the doors. *So much for that idea.*

"Come on." Blythe beckoned to Rebecca. "We'll go outside while we can."

Out of any other ideas, I followed them out into the daylight. The sky was overcast, but at least it wasn't raining, so I didn't have to spend any longer inside that bizarre hall. Blythe's manner suggested she didn't want me hanging around her sister, so I scanned the garden and spotted Robin Wildwood heading off into the maze of hedges alone. *Where's she going?*

An instant later, a fluffy red tail popped up and followed her—Tansy, her familiar.

Quickening my pace, I caught up to Robin before she vanished around a corner. "Hey. You said Tansy was watching when Coral Vervain went off alone?"

"Yeah." She came to a halt, her gaze drifting back towards the house as if she were assessing whether anyone else had seen her slipping away. "She did, but she was too high up in the tree to see if anyone else followed before Rebecca did. I wish she'd been able to get closer."

Tansy squeaked as though in agreement, her fluffy red tail waving back and forth.

"You can understand her, then?" I looked between them, taking in the slightest changes in facial expressions that indicated they understood each other in a deeper way than most witches and their familiars, and made a mental note to keep her off the suspect list. A cold-blooded killer wouldn't have such a strong bond with their familiar, surely.

"Yeah, thanks to my family's gift," she said. "I can understand pretty much every animal, and vice versa, but Tansy and I have known each other the longest."

Tansy squeaked again, scurrying onto her witch's shoulder.

"I didn't know that was a possible coven gift," I said. "Must come in handy."

"It does, but it sounds like you have a useful talent too."

"I wish I could say it'd helped me find the culprit," I admitted. "Perhaps I shouldn't have warned everyone I'd be able to tell if they lied, but I didn't know how else to convince them to let me to stay."

"Tricky." She pursed her lips. "Most of the Head Witches are probably accomplished enough at telling half-truths that it might not have made a difference if you'd kept it hidden."

"Yeah... have you ever met Jodie Atwater before?" I asked. "Or Catherine Oakley?"

"No," she said. "The truth is I'm as new to this as

Rebecca is. More, possibly. I have no idea who the killer might be."

True. "Well, you're off the suspect list," I quipped. "That just leaves about a dozen others. Or more, if I go by the process of elimination."

"The four other Head Witches who came from my region probably didn't do it," said Robin. "Or... ah, here's my mother. You can safely strike her off the list too."

I turned around in time to see Lady Wildwood approaching us. She halted in front of her daughter, giving me an appraising look. "You have an interesting skill."

"Erm... thanks." Lady Wildwood seemed a touch over-bearing, based on my observations so far, but surely Robin would know if her mother had any reason to want to murder any of the other Head Witches.

"Yes," she went on. "Some covens employ witches with similar gifts to yours to work with the police on cases like this."

"Really?" I wasn't sure how she wanted me to respond to that. "I didn't know."

"If you don't mind my asking, did you inherit the gift from your coven?"

Ah. That's what has her intrigued.

"Erm, it was from my mother's side." I kept my answer vague. "Her coven doesn't exist anymore."

"Which coven would that be?"

I'd really hoped to avoid this question. "Wildflower. No relation to Wildwood, I assume."

"No." She wrinkled her nose. "Certainly not. Given their unfortunate reputation, I'm rather glad of it."

Ack. She does know the name.

"Mother," said Robin. "That's enough."

Does Robin know too? If not, then I hoped she wouldn't

press for details, because I really didn't need to enlighten anyone else on the links between my mother's coven and Rebecca's mother's ambitions. Since Lady Wildwood carried the distinct air of someone hoping to talk to her daughter alone, I politely excused myself and headed towards the coven's headquarters.

I'd wondered if Madame Grey had come outside, but instead, Nathan beckoned for me to join him near the front gates. "Blair, the hunters have asked me to help guard the property and keep an eye on the suspects."

"They have?" I blinked at him. "They know you left the hunters, right?"

"Yes, but they need assistance, given the size of the coven's headquarters and the number of suspects present. I'm going to watch the front gates to make sure nobody gets out."

"Okay." Something in his tone made the slightest hint of panic stir inside me. What had they said to him? "And? What else?"

He drew in a breath. "The fact is if I'm seen talking to you or any of the others, they'll assume I'm biased and refuse to tell me anything. Including whatever might be going on in their jail."

My mouth dropped open. "What? Do you mean you have to pretend you have no connection to any of the witches at all?"

"No pretending," he said. "I won't hide our relationship, but it's best if we don't talk about the investigation where we can be overheard. It's the only way to prove to them that I'm not biased."

"I understand."

That didn't mean anything had changed between us. Intellectually, I knew that, but of all the things I'd expected this murder case to involve, the possibility of being separated from Nathan had never crossed my mind. We hadn't been pushed onto opposite sides of a conflict in a long time, and even though I knew it was temporary, it hurt like hell to see him walk away.

6

———————

I allowed myself one minute to mope before returning to join the other witches. Madame Grey still hadn't returned from the meeting room, which left me to avoid Lady Wildwood and anyone else who might want to ask awkward questions alluding to how I'd got my unusual magical gift. Even without mentioning the fairy part, bringing up the Wildflower Coven was a great way to land myself at the top of the suspect list *and* further implicate Rebecca by association too.

No, my best bet was to do some investigating of my own. I'd have an excuse to talk to Nathan *and* a way to be useful, and I might find it easier to unearth the other witches' secrets in a less high-pressure setting than the meeting room.

I looked for someone who might be open to chatting, and my gaze landed on Meredith Norwood. She was talking to Stephanie Underhill, whose already-sour expression morphed into a scowl when she saw me looking at them. As I approached, Stephanie stepped between me and Meredith.

"You're the lie detector," said Stephanie. "You know, if you're going to talk yourself up, you might at least be useful."

What was her problem? "I wasn't trying to talk myself up. I just hoped that I might be able to help."

"Well, you were wrong."

I blinked in surprise at her level of open hostility, though perhaps I should have expected it, given that I was an undisputed outsider. "What do you suggest I should have done instead?"

"Stayed at home," she said bluntly. "Rather than inserting yourself into business that isn't any concern of yours."

"Whatever happens to Rebecca *is* my concern." As Stephanie wasn't a Head Witch, she hadn't been on my radar as a potential suspect, but her attitude annoyed me enough that I had to wonder what her problem was. "It's too late to turn back now."

She narrowed her eyes at me. "It was too late the instant a sceptre chose a child as Head Witch."

My mouth parted. "What do you mean?" She couldn't possibly have known this would happen, right?

"The moment Rebecca was chosen as Head Witch, everyone who stood to gain from her position would have started scheming. I would have thought you of all people would be aware of that."

"I am." Okay, she definitely had a personal grudge against at least one of us. "Which coven are you from?"

"The Hollyhock Coven," she said. "Aveline Hollyhock is my coven leader, but she declined to attend the meeting."

Oh. I'd known Aveline had spurned Madame Grey's invitation, but I hadn't known a potential rival to Rebecca would be attending in her place. "You didn't try out as Head Witch yourself, did you?"

"No," she said. "I knew that Aveline was likely to be chosen again, so there was no point in putting in the effort."

That was true, but there was something in her words that snagged against my lie-sensing power, as if she wasn't telling the full truth.

"Why didn't you try out, then?" I pressed. "Last Samhain? You must have known Aveline was on the brink of retiring."

"That ability of yours is telling you that I'm lying, is it?" she guessed. "You can believe whatever you want about me, but I knew that wasn't the right time for me to try out for the position. I'd expected her to retire before then, but she didn't."

"So... you hoped Aveline would retire or die and let you slip in without it having to come to a vote." That made more sense, though it was kind of lazy on her part. Then again, it might have kept her alive, considering how murderous the other candidates who'd wanted to take Aveline's place had turned out to be.

"Not in the slightest," she said. "Rather, I hoped the vote would be confined to my own coven and town. Not... elsewhere."

Meaning Fairy Falls? If I had to guess, I would say her annoyance stemmed from someone from a different town and coven taking our region's Head Witch title rather than a personal grudge against Rebecca in particular. But while she might not have killed Coral Vervain herself, that didn't mean she didn't stand to gain from Rebecca's downfall.

Stephanie stepped aside without another word and left my route to Meredith clear. By now, though, the other witch had disappeared. I spotted two hunters standing outside the front gates, but I'd lost sight of Nathan too. Maybe it was for the best, given that we had to keep our distance from each other.

I walked through the grounds to get my bearings. More hunters stood outside the back gates, giving me the distinct feeling of being trapped, despite the spaciousness of the gardens surrounding the house.

After I'd circled the house, I found my steps taking me towards the scene of the crime. Coral's body had been moved, of course, but the hedges looked the same as they had beforehand, without a single leaf out of place. I didn't know what I expected to find—proof of someone's guilt, perhaps, however unlikely it might seem.

Rustling came from the bushes at the end of the clearing. I trod that way, my heartbeat quickening.

Brenna Thorngrove leapt up with a yelp of surprise. "Sorry, didn't hear you over there."

"Neither did I." I pressed a hand to my thumping heart. "Are you looking for something?"

If I had to guess, I would say she'd come to look around the murder scene, too, but why was she hiding under a bush?

"No. I dropped an earring, but I don't think it's here."

Lie. My mouth parted, and the merest hint of fear flickered in her eyes before she turned and scurried away.

I looked under the bushes where she'd been crouching but found nothing. What was she playing at? Brenna wasn't a Head Witch, so might she have decided to take it upon herself to investigate too?

I followed her path back to the other Head Witches, but she'd long since vanished elsewhere in the garden. I did spot Madame Grey finally leaving the building, so I hurried over to the steps to waylay her before she could get ambushed by anyone else.

"Madame Grey," I said in a low voice. "Can I talk to you alone?"

"Of course, Blair." She walked alongside me, heading for a corner of the garden near a fountain. "What is it?"

"Blythe told me that her mother has contact with the outside world," I blurted. "She's been having visitors to her cell... including Coral Vervain, apparently. Even Nathan didn't know."

She raised a brow. "I take it he does now?"

"Now I've told him, yes, but I don't know why Blythe didn't tell you either—"

"To protect her sister, of course," she said in a surprisingly calm tone. "It's entirely understandable that she'd want to make sure her sister was unaware that their mother was trying to contact the outside world, since it would do nothing but distract her at a time like this."

"But keeping it a secret from the rest of us?" That still didn't sit right with me. "Especially with people out to target Rebecca. Blythe might at least have told *you*."

"I agree, but that won't change the facts," she said. "We have to work with the situation as it is and deal with the murder before anything else."

I frowned. "You don't think it's relevant that the murder victim might have recently had contact with Rebecca's mother? Why would Coral visit her in the first place? Were they allies?"

"Not to my knowledge," Madame Grey said. "The contact Coral had with Mrs Dailey before her arrest is tangential at best. Several others present at the meeting were former allies of hers, so being acquainted is not an automatic proof of guilt."

"Maybe not, but... well, I spoke to Lady Wildwood earlier, and she asked which coven I got my gift from. I wonder how many others knew." When she gave me an expectant look, I added, "I mean, I'm connected to Mrs Dailey, too, via my mother's coven. Might the person who set Rebecca up have wanted me to take the fall as well?"

"It's possible," she said, "but we'd need concrete proof. Have you been able to find any more clues?"

My face flushed. Was she disappointed in me for not making more progress on finding the killer? "I... I did speak to Stephanie Underhill. I didn't realise she was part of the Hollyhock Coven, and it sounds like she was hoping for Aveline Hollyhock to retire and to seize the chance to snag the sceptre. She has a reason to want Rebecca to step down, doesn't she?"

"Stephanie is highly unlikely to be the killer. She doesn't have any close friendships or alliances with the other Head Witches that I'm aware of."

"Oh." Whoever else might have stood to gain from Rebecca's downfall, it was ultimately a Head Witch who'd murdered Coral Vervain. "I really think this link with Mrs Dailey is worth looking into, though."

"Not yet," she said. "Don't forget that the hunters haven't yet designated Rebecca as a major suspect. If we push them towards her mother, then they're more likely to pay her attention."

I hadn't even thought of that. "All right. Ah—I also found Brenna Thorngrove at the murder scene. I think she might have been looking for clues herself. Might it be worth talking to her again?"

Before she could reply, a low yowling noise rang out, and Rebecca's familiar, Toast, came sprinting past and disappeared under a nearby bush.

Rebecca followed a moment later, her expression distraught. "I have to talk to you both."

"Weren't you with Blythe?" I didn't see her sister anywhere. Had Blythe ditched her again?

"She went to make a call," she said. "I have... I got a message from my mother."

"From—who?" I stared at her. "That's impossible. She's not allowed to contact anyone, is she?"

"I don't think there's a rule stopping her from sending letters." She held up a crumpled piece of paper.

I stared at the paper as she unfolded it in her shaking hands. "Who gave you that?"

"Someone gave it to Toast," she whispered. "I don't know who, but... look."

I read the words on the page. *I heard about the unfortunate situation at the coven meeting. Might I offer you the chance to talk to me so we can discuss our options?*

I didn't know if it was her mother's handwriting, but the tone was entirely typical of Mrs Dailey. How dare she contact her daughter after the trauma she'd already caused her? I stood rigid, disbelief mingling with sudden fury. "Who exactly is your sister talking to? Why'd she run off on you at a time like this?"

"I don't know," she said. "I had to get away from the others. They... they can't know about this."

"Is Blythe trying to contact your mother herself?"

I made to approach the house again, but Madame Grey said, "Blair. Stop."

Her sharp tone brought me to a halt, and I spun around. "I can't let this stand."

"Please don't do anything rash," she said softly. "All that will achieve is to give the others a reason to look badly upon us or on Fairy Falls as a whole. That includes the hunters as well as the witches."

"I'm not planning on shouting from the rooftops, but something has to be done." I lowered my voice. "Blythe has contacts in the hunters' jail. I'm sure. She can't have known her mother had visitors any other way. What else might she have lied about?"

"Visitors?" Rebecca's eyes widened in horror. "She told you that?"

I dipped my head. "Sorry, Rebecca. I just found out a few minutes ago. I wanted to ask Madame Grey before anything else."

Rebecca made a choked noise. "People are talking to her? To our mother?"

"Yes, but Blythe didn't say anything about her being able to deliver letters to anyone," I said. "We need to find the person responsible for giving Toast that letter. I'd suggest asking the hunters, but... well, it might have been one of them who did it." I saw no point in understating the level of trouble we might be in, though seeing Rebecca's open terror brought another wave of fury.

"Precisely why we can't tell them," Madame Grey agreed. "Now do you see the position we're in, Blair?"

"I already did, but we're taking a major risk here." Keeping secrets from the people in charge of the investigation did not seem a wise idea, but what choice did we have? "Also, if Mrs Dailey is trying to interfere, then I wouldn't put it past her to coerce or trick the hunters into arresting the wrong person. Whether that's Rebecca or not."

"I'll see to it that that doesn't happen," said Madame Grey. "Like I said, it would be a lot easier if the real culprit were exposed."

My shoulders slumped. "I'm trying, but nobody is telling any obvious lies. And it'd help if I knew where to start. Is there anyone else you've outright struck from your list of suspects?"

"The Wildwoods and everyone from their region," she said promptly. "As for the rest, the likely culprit varies, depending on whether one wants to believe that the murder was intended to discredit Rebecca or she was simply in the wrong place at the wrong time."

"If the latter, then it's aimed at the witches' council as a whole?" I guessed. "I'm not so sure it can be one or the other. It's more likely to be both."

Someone had delivered that letter to Rebecca, too, but exposing them wouldn't be easy. I'd need to talk to Nathan, at the very least, if I wanted to find out who might have connections in the hunters' jail—and how to stop them from abusing their power any further.

"That would be typical." Rebecca's hand clenched around the scrap of paper. "What am I supposed to do now?"

"Of the witches here, who has the most to gain from you being jailed?" I asked her. "Stephanie Underhill, for one, had her eye on Aveline's position, but I don't know that she'd go as far as to set you up for murder."

She hadn't said anything that'd tripped up my suspicions, but her disdain towards Rebecca had been notable—not to mention towards *me*.

"I don't know," she murmured. "I didn't realise she was looking at Aveline's position *or* that she'd be here. There's so much I thought I knew but didn't."

At that moment, I spotted Blythe approaching us, and Madame Grey leaned closer to me. "Remember to keep your priorities straight, Blair."

She wanted me to ignore the fact that Blythe had potentially endangered all of us by keeping her mother's activity a secret from everyone else.

"All right, but if she refuses to share who she spoke to, then she's clearly not committed to helping any of us."

"I don't think that will be a problem, Blair." She addressed Rebecca in a low voice, the words too quiet for me to hear, before she departed in several quick strides.

Blythe reached our side a moment later, and I clamped down on my instinct to reprimand her. Ignoring me, she addressed her sister. "She told you? About our mother?"

"Yes, I did," I replied, keeping my tone even. "I told Madame Grey too. Given the timing of the letter, I doubt I'd have been able to avoid it for long. I'm guessing one of the hunters was responsible for delivering it into your sister's hands."

"I think so too," Blythe muttered. "Someone delivered that message, and they were sneaky about it."

"Exactly," I said. "Who did you speak to on the phone? Someone who might be able to help?"

"No." She glanced at Rebecca. "Ah... it's just someone who keeps an eye on the hunters from a distance. They didn't know about this."

True. "I'll take your word on that, but Blythe, if there's anything you know that might help, then you have to tell Madame Grey, at the very least."

"I know." She lowered her gaze. "I didn't think anything like this would happen. I also have no idea who offered to deliver that letter."

"How did she expect you to reply?" I asked Rebecca. "Even if you wanted to accept her so-called offer, did she think you'd write a note and give it to your familiar in the hopes that the wrong person didn't pick it up?"

"I don't know," she said. "Toast was sitting by the back

gates when they gave it to him, so maybe if he returned to the same spot..."

"Not exactly foolproof." I shook my head. "I think she's desperate. Even if your mother planned this, it's nothing like her usual schemes."

"Don't speak too soon," said Blythe. "She's limited in what she can do from jail, but she has allies even now."

No kidding. Moreover, Mrs Dailey's offer raised another possibility. What if the killer had wanted to set Rebecca up so that she had no choice but to call on her mother for help and therefore open herself back up to Mrs Dailey's influence?

If that was the case, then perhaps the killer was her mother's ally, not her enemy.

7

"Blythe," I said, "who among the people in this house was allied with your mother? Do you know?"

Despite her attitude problems, I wanted to make a little effort to work with her at the very least, especially as I had few allies here who were free to speak for themselves. Madame Grey had enough to deal with already, while Nathan had to play nice with the hunters to make any progress.

"Her former allies?" Blythe scoffed. "Nobody here would ever admit to supporting her."

"Coral Vervain visited her in jail, you said," I pressed. "Anyone else?"

"I have no idea," she said. "I can list her former supporters, sure, but that doesn't mean they'd admit to currently being in touch, given the circumstances."

True. At least she'd stopped skirting the truth around me, if nothing else. "Can't you dive into their thoughts and find out if there's still some lingering loyalty?"

"No," she said. "Not the ones who've trained themselves to resist their minds being read, which includes almost all of the Head Witches."

"See, that's suspicious enough on its own," I said. "Nobody visits a prisoner as controversial as Mrs Dailey unless they have a very good reason. And on that note, you spoke to someone on the phone, didn't you? Did they share anything else about any of the witches here who might have paid her a visit?"

Blythe glowered at me, but Rebecca gave her a pleading look. "Tell us. It might help."

"Fine," she growled under her breath. "Nathalie Alder visited our mother recently, and she's one of the people whose minds I was unable to read."

"She's not a Head Witch." I thought back and recalled the dark-skinned witch who'd been questioned along with the others who'd come here with Coral Vervain. "I guess she might know something, though, if she spoke to Mrs Dailey. If you don't want to talk to her, then I can go alone. One of us should stay with Rebecca at all times."

"Did Madame Grey say you could take charge?" Blythe sniffed. "You don't have a clue what you're doing."

Just when I thought we'd begun to make progress. "No, she said we weren't to argue with each other and to focus on getting answers. If you still want an argument, I'm sure someone else will be willing. I bet Jodie Atwater would love to fight you."

"That's not what I meant," she muttered. "You have a tendency to jump head first into situations without considering the consequences, and that's what we least need at the moment."

"I know exactly what the consequences will be if we don't find the killer," I countered. "Besides, Madame Grey wants us *both* to find them, and if we can expose whoever gave Rebecca that note, too, so much the better."

Rebecca cleared her throat. "I'd like to have some say in this too."

"Of course," I said. "What do you want to do? I don't think it's a good idea to tell any of the hunters about that letter, but it's up to you."

"I'm not telling them a thing," she said. "I'll destroy it first."

"I'll do it," Blythe and I offered at the same time.

Rebecca looked between us, hesitating with the paper outstretched in her hand, so I motioned for her to give it to Blythe.

As she handed it over, Madame Grey returned at speed. "Rebecca, you've been called in to be questioned next."

Rebecca stiffened. "Should have seen this coming."

"Good luck," I whispered to her. "We'll wait outside the room."

Blythe didn't argue, for a wonder, so the pair of us flanked Rebecca through the oak doors into the entrance hall. From there, two hunters took over and steered Rebecca into a classroom which they must have picked out to use as their interrogation room. The rest of the entrance hall seemed to have shuffled itself around again, and a tall staircase that I was positive hadn't been there earlier dominated the centre.

Blythe ignored the two hunters guarding the questioning room and positioned herself outside to wait for her sister, but there was no chance we could talk privately in here.

"How long will the questioning take? Do you know?" I asked her.

"Ten minutes," she said. "Feel free to return to the party."

"That was the plan." I might have said more but not with the hunters glowering at the pair of us from outside the door. While I didn't entirely trust Blythe not to ignore Madame Grey's instructions for us to work together, she seemed to have learned her lesson about leaving Rebecca on her own. "See you later."

After I left the house, I lingered at the top of the stone stairs for a moment, my gaze skimming over the witches gathered in the garden until I spotted Nathalie talking to Jodie Atwater near one of the fountains. The latter, I had no desire to speak to, though if I did want to ask Nathalie about her secret visits to the hunters' prison, I should probably come up with a way to bring up the subject that wouldn't end badly. One could never predict how someone would react to being called out on their trips to visit a notorious criminal, but there really was no delicate way to approach the subject. Blythe's claims that she couldn't read Nathalie's mind didn't help either.

Realising I was drawing attention by awkwardly hovering at the top of the stairs, I hastily descended into the garden and belatedly remembered Rebecca's familiar, whom we'd left hiding under the bushes. I hadn't gone two steps in that direction before Meredith crossed my path.

"Hey, Blair," she said. "Everything all right? Rebecca's being questioned, right?"

"Yes." What was her angle? I really couldn't tell. It was safe to say she wasn't exchanging letters with Mrs Dailey in jail, though. "Shouldn't take too long."

"No, I expect not," she said. "I saw you talking to some of the others. Trying to catch them in a lie?"

Why did she want to know? It shouldn't surprise me that someone had guessed what I was doing, but I could no more trust her than I could any of the other witches present.

"Not a bad plan," she added. "I guess you probably want the killer found for Rebecca's sake."

I made a noncommittal noise. Meredith hadn't done anything that tripped my suspicions, but I could only imagine what Blythe would say if I tried bringing anyone else into our investigation.

"Anyway, I should head off," she said. "Good luck with your search."

She walked away, leaving me wondering if she'd been inviting me to confide in her and I'd bushed her off. Before I could decide whether to follow or not, Robin came into view around a corner. Upon seeing me, she faltered for an instant before approaching me. "Hey, Blair."

"Hey," I said. "Something up?"

She drew in a breath. "Uh. So, the first thing I wanted to say is that Tansy didn't mean to eavesdrop on you."

"On me?" My heart lurched. "When?"

"C'mon, we can talk over here." She circled a hedge, giving me little choice but to follow her. If she'd overheard my conversation with Rebecca—including the threatening note—then what should I do? Robin wasn't a suspect of mine, but that didn't mean she couldn't inadvertently give something away in front of the others.

When she stopped, I asked, "What did Tansy overhear? Why was she eavesdropping on people to begin with?"

"To figure out what's going on with those hunters," she said. "The paranormal hunters aren't active in our region, so I don't have much experience with them. I know my grandmother kicked them out—she was the last Head Witch, before me—so I figured there must be some unpleasant history between the hunters and the covens."

Tansy herself popped her little head out of the nearby hedge and jumped onto Robin's shoulder, squeaking in her ear.

"You had her eavesdropping on the hunters?" I guessed. "Risky, that."

"Not just them," said Robin. "The other witches too. She ended up over by those hedges."

My heart gave another dive when she pointed at the very corner where I'd been talking to Madame Grey—and then to Rebecca and her sister. "What did she hear?"

"That someone is trying to blackmail Rebecca," Robin said. "Rebecca's own mother, in fact. From what my mum said, it sounds like Mrs Dailey was involved in some kind of attempted coup on the leading coven in your town, and she was in league with those hunters. And now she's in jail. Do I have that right?"

"Yes... mostly." I scrambled to find an easy way to explain that wouldn't land my allies in hot water. "The hunters here aren't supposed to have anything to do with Rebecca's mother. Also, if you overheard us talking, you know Rebecca is never going to accept her offer, right?"

If the others found out the offer existed at all, it meant bad news for Rebecca.

"No, of course she isn't," she said. "For the record, I haven't told anyone, not even my mother. She doesn't like my sending Tansy to eavesdrop on people, but how else are we supposed to find out who the killer is? No offence. I know you're trying."

"You're not supposed to know that either. What else did she overhear?"

My lie-sensing power apparently had nothing on Robin's

familiar, and I had to admit that it was a little humiliating to be outdone by a talking squirrel. Though no one except Robin could understand her. Tansy squeaked a couple of times, and Robin nodded. "Most of what she heard was irrelevant gossip, except when she ran into you and Madame Grey. I had no idea Rebecca's family was worse than mine, but it sounds like her sister had it much easier. She left her sister in that horror show?"

"I wouldn't exactly say that. I don't know if even Blythe knew how bad the manipulation was." I didn't know why, but I felt oddly compelled to defend Blythe, regardless of her behaviour. "Anyway, it's not entirely a surprise that Mrs Dailey is still trying to do the same from a jail cell, but I don't know who delivered that note on her behalf."

"Does Blythe? It sounds like she's not telling you everything." At another squeak from Tansy, she added, "And is your boyfriend *with* the hunters?"

My shoulders slumped. "Nathan was a hunter before we met, but he works for Fairy Falls's security team now. When he updated our local police on Coral's murder, the hunters barged in and invited themselves here. He's playing nice with them for the purposes of finding out whether any of their group is secretly in league with a certain high-security prisoner—and delivering letters now, apparently. Also, if you tell anyone that, you'll get both of us arrested."

"I can keep a secret," she said. "So can Tansy. My mother can't, which is why we aren't going to tell her, but I don't think she wants Rebecca arrested for a crime she didn't commit either."

"At least you know she's innocent," I muttered. "I can't figure out the hunters' angle on this. The ones who aren't in league with Mrs Dailey, that is. It's obvious they wanted to come and assert their authority over the covens, but if they have any suspects of their own, they certainly aren't going to tell *me* who they are."

"But Nathan will, right?" she asked.

"I hope so." I didn't doubt him, but the fact that someone had slipped a letter from Mrs Dailey through a locked gate none of us was able to get through had shaken me more than I wanted to admit. "If Tansy is going to eavesdrop on people, can you send her after the hunters next?"

"Sure," she said. "Which hunters, though? The ones doing the interrogations? Might be hard for her to get into the room."

"No, I doubt they'd have brought the note from inside the house," I said. "It's more likely to be the ones outside the gates."

Tansy squeaked in apparent agreement.

"Worth a try," said Robin. "Tansy, can you keep an eye on the hunters at the gates and see if they talk to anyone else?"

Tansy gave another squeak and scampered away along the hedges. I wished I could understand her myself so I didn't have to use Robin as an intermediary if I wanted to find out whether her familiar had overheard anything important, but as long as Robin kept quiet as she'd promised, then nobody else needed to know what she'd discovered.

"Can I ask you a question or two?" asked Robin. "About the hunters, I mean."

"Er..." She already knew far more than I'd wanted to tell anyone, and while Madame Grey wouldn't be thrilled, at least she'd already put Robin and her family on the short list of non-suspects. I wouldn't have anything to lose from talking to her. "I don't mind. Ask away."

"The hunters are supposed to police paranormals,

right?" she asked. "Who sets the standards? Or are they independent?"

"They're independent of the covens, but they have their own level of authority," I said. "They run most of the paranormal prisons, for a start. They think they're impartial because they don't belong to a specific community or group, which is technically true, but since a lot of their job involves chasing dangerous paranormal criminals, they tend to tar us all with the same brush. I've run into them a few times since I first moved into the paranormal world."

"What? You weren't born into this?"

Too late, I remembered what she *didn't* know—namely, most of my history with the hunters and the paranormal world. "No, I moved to Fairy Falls a year ago. That's how I met Rebecca—her mother kept her at home because of her magical abilities, so she was behind on her schooling. We take classes together."

Her eyes rounded in understanding. "Right. I get it. So, the hunters have always been around?"

"Around Fairy Falls? Yes." I paused. "I suppose you want to know how I ended up dating one of them?"

"Among other things," she said. "If it's not relevant, you don't have to tell me."

"Nathan hasn't been an active hunter since we've known one another," I clarified. "Some of his family members are, and Nathan keeps in contact with them to get updates on certain goings-on."

"You were supposed to know if this Mrs Dailey had contact with the outside world, then?"

"Yeah, we were," I said. "She tried to manipulate her daughter from behind bars once before. In fact, she schemed with the former head of the local branch of hunters, who turned out to secretly be a paranormal himself."

"You know... that rings a bell," she said. "My mother mentioned something about a recent scandal and a head of a local hunters branch resigning after being found to be committing fraud, but she didn't make it sound nearly as exciting."

"Being caught up in it was more terrifying than exciting," I admitted. "Especially for Rebecca. She hadn't been Head Witch for five minutes before her mother tried to take charge, though it's not like anyone predicted an eleven-year-old would be chosen as Head Witch."

"Not even her mother, I bet," she said knowingly.

"No, but she shouldn't be able to reach her former allies or supporters," I said. "If she has someone passing notes around, it can only be one of the hunters."

"AKA the people who are supposed to be investigating Coral Vervain's death," she said. "Oh boy."

"Exactly."

"Tansy will tell me right away if she hears anything suspicious," she said. "As for the hunters... why would they support someone like her? Mrs Dailey, I mean."

"She had this big scheme to depose the ruling coven and put herself in charge," I said. "She recruited the hunters as allies by promising them more influence and control over the rest of the paranormal community. As long as she could lord it over the other witches, she didn't care what they did to anyone else."

"Wow, she wasn't short on ambition, then," she commented. "I suppose having a Head Witch on her side would enable her to undermine the others."

"I don't know that she ever had a definite plan for her

daughter," I said. "If she's somehow involved in this murder, though, she must have concocted one."

Her eyes rounded. "You think Coral's death was part of the blackmail? To force Rebecca to accept her help or else get arrested by the hunters?"

"I don't know, to be honest." With Mrs Dailey not here in person, I could only speculate. "If it's a setup, not all the hunters will be in on it."

"I suppose the hunters would have a lot to gain from getting rid of the covens," she said. "And the Head Witches too. It's a weird system to begin with, since we're all chosen by an object and not voted in."

I raised a brow. "I mean, you're not wrong, but you were chosen too. You're here."

"I don't have much choice," she said in a low voice. "I wasn't supposed to claim my sceptre. My mother always thought she'd be Head Witch instead, but when my aunt tried to take the title by force, I grabbed the sceptre, and voila. It's mine now, until it decides otherwise."

Now that she'd described the process, it did sound like an absurd way to pick someone to represent an entire region of witches. "Yeah, Rebecca was in a similar situation. Someone stole the sceptre from the last Head Witch on Samhain, when it was due to pick a new wielder, and there were a few murders... or faked deaths. It was a bit of a mess."

"Sounds it," she said. "The hunters didn't have a hand in that one?"

"Not that time," I replied. "After Rebecca was chosen, I bet someone told her mother right away."

"Like the hunters." She blew out a breath. "I see the bind you're in."

"Hence why I need to find the real killer before the

hunters have the chance to make any more trouble than they already have."

"Tansy and I will do our best to help," she said. "I should get back to my mother before she comes looking for me. Oh, and I won't tell her any of this."

"Thanks," I said, glad that at least one person was on my side.

I just hoped the next conversation that Tansy overheard would point us to the killer.

$$8$$

____

The hunters continued their questioning throughout the rest of the afternoon.

Rebecca returned after ten minutes or so, looking relieved. "They didn't seem to suspect me any more than anyone else. I don't think they did, anyway."

"That's good news," I said. "I hope they're actually doing their jobs. They didn't drop any hints about...?"

"The note?" She lowered her voice. "No, but they can't have been responsible for delivering any messages while they were questioning suspects at the same time."

But some of the other hunters might be involved. We couldn't rule out that possibility, and neither could we drop our guard.

Blythe, who'd accompanied her sister, said, "I wouldn't rule anything out."

"What did they ask you, then?" I asked Rebecca. "They know you found the body?"

"Yeah... and they did ask a few questions about our plans to talk after the meeting. I made it clear that Coral and

I didn't know each other before today and that I have no idea how to use the curse that killed her."

"Good." It seemed too good to be true, in fact, and it didn't surprise me when Blythe shook her head.

"The hunters always have an angle," she said. "One of them planted that letter on your familiar."

"I haven't forgotten," said Rebecca. "Isn't it better than their deciding I'm guilty and locking me up, though?"

"Of course it is," I said with a pointed look at her sister. "It sounds like they're giving everyone a fair shot to explain themselves. If someone among their group is scheming, it's not the ones doing the questioning. That's a starting point."

"For what?" Blythe asked. "I thought you were looking for the killer, not nosing around the hunters. Unless you already found out who it is."

"No, I haven't, but I did speak to Robin." I remembered how displeased Blythe would be when she learned how much I'd shared with Robin. I wouldn't be able to keep it from them forever, though, and Robin's familiar had been the one to overhear our chat. All I'd done was clarify what she'd found out.

"What about her?" asked Blythe. "You didn't tell her, did you?"

"She guessed, but she's on our side." I spoke quickly to prevent her from interrupting. "She wanted to talk to me about the hunters because she's never met them before—they aren't active in her area, so she wanted to learn how they operated. I didn't tell her everything, but I gave her enough information to know they aren't to be trusted. She already had her familiar spying on them, so I asked her to let me know if she finds anything out."

"We can't let anyone else in on this," Blythe said. "You shouldn't have talked to her."

"Bit late now," I said. "Relax. She promised not to tell anyone, and she and her mother are the only people who can understand Tansy. Their family gift lets her communicate with any animal."

Rebecca paled. "Really? But... that means she can ask Toast who gave him that note."

"Good point." I looked at Blythe. "It's worth trying, right?"

Never mind that she knew who the note was from as well as I did, surely—this might be our chance to catch Mrs Dailey's allies in the act.

Blythe shook her head. "No. It's too risky."

"Robin can talk directly to Toast without involving anyone else," Rebecca pressed. "I bet the hunters never thought of that, did they?"

"Exactly," I said. "I bet Madame Grey would give us permission if she asked. Where is Toast, anyway?"

"I don't know." Rebecca's face fell. "I haven't seen him since before my interview. I told him he could wander around the garden because I know he doesn't like being cooped up, and last I saw, he was hiding under the hedges."

"Right, of course." I headed towards the area where I'd last seen him, but it would have been easy to spot the large orange cat even from a distance. "I was going to look for him earlier, but I got distracted."

"Toast?" Rebecca crouched down near the hedge and called out her familiar's name. "Toast?"

No response came, though several witches turned in our direction, including Robin and her mother. While Rebecca continued to search under the hedges, I approached the pair of them at a stride. "Have either of you seen Rebecca's familiar? He seems to have wandered off."

"The big orange cat?" asked Robin. "No, but I'll keep an eye out for him. Tansy will too."

"I expect he's gone hunting or to entertain himself," said Lady Wildwood. "When was the last time you saw him?"

"Before I was questioned," Rebecca caught me up, breathless. "I'm sure he'll show up."

We continued our search of the garden, asking anyone we passed if they'd seen Toast and checking behind every flower bed and underneath every hedge. No signs of him materialised even as we walked right up to the back of the garden, Rebecca growing more and more panicked every time she called out and didn't get a response.

Where is her familiar? Did someone take him? Maybe the hunters had taken her lack of a response as a refusal and had taken new measures to convince her to reply to her mother's offer. The timing of his disappearance was too suspicious to overlook.

My circuit of the garden took me close enough to the gates to spot Nathan talking to one of the hunters standing outside. Despite my better instincts telling me to walk away, part of me wondered what they were discussing. Nathan showed no signs of having seen me, but I had no doubt that he'd have to pretend to be fully on board with the hunters' plans in order to find out what they knew—including whom Mrs Dailey had contact with.

"There's no precedent for this," I heard him saying to the hunters. "You must know that this unfortunate turn of events isn't a reflection on the Knotgrass Coven. The odds are high that the murder would have taken place no matter which coven held the meeting."

"But it's the Knotgrass Coven who failed to prevent it," one of the hunters replied.

"You can't assume any others would have done better,"

he said. "The focus should be on the killer, not the host coven."

"I don't see why we can't do both," said the hunter. "In fact, Linda has all but requested it. It's a clear indication of why we should be the ones calling the shots."

Were the hunters already making plans to step in and overtake the local covens? Even if they were, it didn't mean they were necessarily linked to Mrs Dailey and her ambitions, though. If I stayed here much longer, they'd spot me, and I didn't see any signs of a large orange cat, so I reluctantly turned away.

Rebecca waited for me beside a fountain, her gaze downcast. "He's not here. He's gone."

"We should look in the house before we raise any alarms," I said to her. "He might have decided to explore inside or wait for you there. In fact, he might be napping in a spot of sunlight."

"Yeah." She chewed on her lower lip. "I'd have thought he would have heard me calling for him, but I guess it's a pretty big house."

"Exactly." I didn't blame her for worrying, but we didn't need to make an already-stressful situation even worse. I kept my panic at the back of my mind as we met Blythe and climbed the steps to the house's front doors.

Blythe stepped up behind us. "I didn't see him go into the house."

"There's more than one way in," I reminded her. "He's got to be somewhere in here."

Even if the hunters had been intending to intimidate us into accepting Mrs Dailey's offer, it would make no sense for them to take away Rebecca's means of replying—unless they'd taken her silence to mean no and reacted accordingly. Handing letters to Rebecca's familiar was the one obvious way to communicate with us without giving away the identities of Mrs Dailey's allies.

No, something didn't add up. I also hadn't seen Madame Grey on our way here, though that wasn't unusual, since she had her own careful balancing act to perform. We certainly weren't supposed to make her life any more difficult by losing Rebecca's familiar.

We circled the main hall and opened the doors one at a time, until a pair of hunters barred our way into the council meeting room.

"What are you doing in here?" asked the hunter on the right, the heavyset man with the shaved head.

"Has either of you seen a cat?" Rebecca asked. "My familiar has wandered off somewhere in here, and I can't find him. He's big and orange."

"No, we haven't seen him," the hunter growled in reply.

"Okay," I said. "Can you let you know if you do? He might be lost, and Rebecca is pretty worried about him."

"We'll let you know."

Lie.

Rebecca nodded. "Thanks. I don't want him to worry about me."

She turned away while I debated calling the hunter out on his untruth. Might he be one of the hunters who was scheming against us? Or could he just not be bothered to look out for missing familiars? I didn't recognise this particular hunter as one of Mrs Dailey's allies, but that didn't prove anything. Maybe I should have asked Robin to send her familiar to spy on the hunters inside the building instead of outside it.

"He's lying," I whispered to Rebecca once we were out of earshot of the hunter. "Not sure why or how, but he is."

She stiffened. "He is? Is he the one who's—"

"I don't know. People tell white lies all the time."

Rebecca lowered her head. "I wish I knew who to trust."

"Robin, for a start." I knew how she felt, though. "She can send her familiar to spy on pretty much anyone without being noticed, and it's handy to have someone only she can understand. Pity we don't—wait." I *did* have someone I could communicate with and nobody else could—kind of, anyway.

"Huh?" asked Rebecca.

"Sky," I said. "My familiar. I bet he can find Toast."

Rebecca's eyes widened. "Is he even here?"

"I haven't seen him since we left Fairy Falls, but he must be around somewhere," I said. "He wouldn't have offered to come with me if he wasn't going to stick around. I can't understand him like Robin can understand her familiar, but if anyone can figure out how to navigate this house, it's him."

"Hope so." Rebecca headed for the front door to join her sister while I looked for a likely place in which to call my familiar without drawing too much attention. I ought to have asked Sky to help us find out what was going on from the start, but I'd genuinely forgotten he was supposed to be here. He'd disappeared before we'd properly left Fairy Falls, and I hadn't seen any signs of him since.

I circled the hedges and found a clear spot in the garden free from any possible eavesdroppers before calling for my familiar.

"Sky," I muttered. "Sky?"

No response came, but that didn't mean he wasn't listening. My cat had a kind of psychic ability which meant he always knew where to come and find me. It was too bad the reverse wasn't true.

"Sky, I need your help." I spoke louder. "We all do."

Please don't tell me my familiar is missing as well. That was all I needed. It was far more likely that he'd wandered off to do his own thing, but his timing was infuriating, to say the least.

Giving up for now, I went to look for Toast again. It was possible I'd overlooked him the first time. The garden was as much of a labyrinth as the house, and every circuit of the hedges brought me to a new place. I halted near a fountain topped with another carving of a witch on a broomstick, and my gaze snagged on an oddly misshapen hedge.

The hedge looked, in fact, as if something solid had been stuffed inside it. I approached, my heart giving a sickening lurch when I spotted a hand sticking out.

Brenna Thorngrove lay sprawled half in and half out of the hedge—dead.

"Help!" The word left my mouth before I could think better of it. "Someone, help!"

Unfortunately, it was Rebecca and Blythe who heard me first and came running into view. Blythe stopped dead at the sight of Brenna Thorngrove's body, while Rebecca went deathly pale.

"She's dead," she whispered. "How?"

"I don't know." I didn't dare get any closer to the body, but questions exploded inside my mind. What had Brenna been doing here alone? How had nobody noticed she was missing?

"Why her?" Rebecca murmured. "I don't understand."

Neither did I. *Who would have killed both Brenna and Coral?* I couldn't for the life of me see a connection between the two victims at all. They weren't from the same coven or even from the same town. *Unless...*

"She was searching the place where Coral died earlier," I said. "I went for a look around the crime scene and found her hiding in a bush. I think she might have been doing some investigating of her own."

Please tell me I wasn't the last person to see her alive. That's all I need. It was bad enough that I'd been the one who'd found her body, let alone that the other two had come here before anyone else had.

"Really?" asked Rebecca. "Maybe she figured out who the killer was."

At that moment, several other witches ran into view.

Catherine Oakley let out a shrill scream at the sight of Brenna's body. "What happened to her?"

"I don't know," I said. "I don't even know how long she's been there."

"Move aside," a hunter called out. "We're in charge here."

The hunters moved in, forcing the crowd to let them through. Two of them lifted Brenna's body out of the hedge and carried her to a free spot on the lawn, while Linda Graham, the leading hunter, surveyed the body. Brenna lay in a limp heap, her limbs splayed. Had she been killed by the same curse that had killed Coral?

"Who found her?" she demanded.

"I did." I tensed when all eyes turned towards me, even though I'd known it was coming.

"The lie detector," said Jodie Atwater, her eyes glittering. "Convenient."

"What's that supposed to mean?" I asked. "I didn't touch Brenna. I don't even know how she died."

"It appears to be the same curse as the one that killed the previous victim," said Linda Graham. "A Head Witch killed her."

Rebecca wasn't here. She'd been inside the house at the time Brenna must have been killed, but Linda's confident tone suggested she'd expected this eventuality. So had the other hunters. They'd been counting on another murder to boost their chances of gaining a new level of authority over the covens, and from the expressions of grim satisfaction on some of their faces, I knew they now had an excuse to do exactly that.

9

The hunters and the witches remained in a standoff over Brenna's body for several minutes, at least until Madame Grey materialised from somewhere nearby. She spoke to the hunters in a low voice, but my relief at the sight of her was tempered by my certainty that even she hadn't seen this coming. Whatever she said to them brought an end to their argument with the witches, and Linda ordered a couple of hunters to move Brenna's body into the house. Meanwhile, the witches moved back to the main part of the garden, in front of the house.

"From now on, there won't be any wandering off alone," Linda Graham told everyone. "You'll all stay within sight of the house."

What now? It had briefly occurred to me that the hunters' distraction might give Rebecca an opportunity to properly search for Toast, but it wouldn't be wise for either of us to wander off alone.

Rebecca shuffled in behind me, one eye on Madame Grey. "We need to tell her about Toast. I know it's bad timing, but the hunters are never going to let us search the house now, and he might be in trouble."

Blythe appeared at her sister's back, and I caught Madame Grey's gaze at least three times before she left the hunters behind and made her way over to the three of us.

"Madame Grey," I whispered. "We need to talk to you alone. It's urgent."

"Whatever it is, I'm sure it can wait," she said brusquely. "Unless it's connected to Brenna's unfortunate death."

"No. Well, possibly," I amended. "Rebecca's familiar is missing, and now we're not allowed to go off alone, we can't find him."

"Have you already searched the house?"

"Most of the downstairs floor," replied Blythe. "Except the parts the hunters have taken over."

"He wasn't in the questioning room," said Rebecca. "I doubt he's in the meeting room, either, but there are other rooms. The house keeps changing."

"Yes, Arabella claims she can't turn off the spell on her house despite the urgency of the situation." Madame Grey pursed her lips. "The garden too. I have little doubt the killer would have found it harder to remain hidden if the hedges didn't move around."

So I hadn't imagined the place being a literal maze. "Yeah... the last time I saw her alive was when she was searching the bushes at the scene of Coral's death."

Maybe she'd figured something out after all, but I had no way of knowing now she was dead. I hadn't liked Brenna much, but I hadn't really suspected her of murdering Coral either. Now it was too late to ask her any questions.

"You don't think she figured out who killed Coral, do you?" asked Rebecca.

"Did she?" Madame Grey's gaze sharpened. "If she did, it

explains why she was targeted herself."

"If she did, she didn't tell me any of her suspicions." I lowered my gaze. "Nobody here is willing to talk. Not to me, at any rate."

And now that I'd discovered Brenna's body, I doubted any of the witches would change their minds in a hurry. A nagging sense of guilt told me I hadn't tried hard enough to find out what Brenna had known, but if the hunters had questioned her, then she evidently hadn't told them anything either.

"What will the hunters do now?" Rebecca asked Madame Grey. "Carry on with the questioning as if nothing happened? Or switch their focus over to Brenna's death instead?"

"That, I'm not entirely sure," she said. "It's their decision. I intend to give them my input, but I'm afraid our opinions matter little to them."

"Yeah." Worry clawed up my throat. "I heard them at the gates, and I'm sure they're hoping this will give them another excuse to grab power from the covens."

"No way," Rebecca said. "They can't."

Madame Grey looked askance at me. "I think that's the least of the possible consequences if these murders remain unresolved, Blair."

As she walked away, I became aware that the crowd had dispersed so much that we'd only draw attention by staying this close to the scene of the crime.

"I'm going to find Nathan," I told Blythe.

"No need," she said. "He's already here."

My heart skipped a beat when I spied him speaking to another hunter at the edge of the garden. I moved towards them, but when our gazes connected, his expression barely showed any recognition. Even though I knew why keeping his distance was necessary for both of us, it stung all the same to see him talking to the hunters in such a familiar way. It might be nothing more than an act, but imagining him reminiscing about old times with the people who had us all on trial didn't help my mood in the slightest.

I shoved the feeling aside with a firm hand. I didn't need to be reassured of his loyalty to me every five minutes, and we'd already agreed to keep our distance for the duration. Yet I had to wonder if he'd heard about Rebecca's letter from her mother... or her missing familiar.

I had to face it—the other hunters weren't going to lift a finger to help, but the longer Toast remained missing, the more stressed Rebecca became, and the higher the chances of her mother making another move against us. Nathan needed to know.

I waited for Linda to walk away before approaching the gates and addressing him. "Nathan, I need to talk to you."

"Not now, Blair." The cool note to his voice hurt more even than seeing him speaking to the hunters, and a feeling of unreality swept over me, as if the ground were shifting under my feet—and not because of one of Arabella Knotgrass's spells, either.

"Rebecca's familiar is missing." My voice shook despite my best efforts. "He's not in the garden, and we aren't allowed to search the entire house. Did... did Madame Grey tell you?"

I meant about the offer Mrs Dailey had made, though I didn't dare so much as allude to it in case anyone else was listening in.

"No, I've been outside all the time," he said. "I'll keep an eye out for Toast, Blair. That's all I can do."

So much for that idea. I doubted he'd be as quick to brush me off if Madame Grey *had* told him that Mrs Dailey was blackmailing Rebecca, but I didn't dare tell him myself with the other hunters close at hand. With my eyes stinging, I turned my back on him and sought out Rebecca and her sister.

"Trouble in paradise?" asked Blythe.

"Excuse me?" I couldn't believe she'd talk so flippantly at a time like this. Dropping my voice, I hissed, "Nathan is spying on the hunters on our behalf in order to find the killer and stop me and your sister from getting arrested. It's nothing personal."

"Doesn't look that way from where I'm standing." She shrugged. "Just an observation."

"It's none of your business." Did she have to choose now to start pushing my buttons? "He's following Madame Grey's orders in staying away from me. Like I'm following her orders to cooperate with you rather than turning you into a hedgehog."

She blinked, amusement glinting in her eyes. "Why a hedgehog?"

"It's the first thing that popped into my head." *Why did it have to be her?* "I only spoke to him because I wanted to know if he'd seen Toast. You know, your sister's missing familiar."

"Guys," said Rebecca. "Cut it out. We have enough problems without you snipping at each other."

She started it was the response to come to mind—childish but true—but I didn't need to be lectured by an eleven-year-old Head Witch to know that this wasn't the time for an argument. As for Blythe, whether her current mood had been triggered by the most recent murder or by the situation in general, she wasn't making it any easier for any of us.

"We do have enough problems," said Blythe. "Like her."

I followed her gaze to Linda Graham, who stood at the foot of the staircase at the front of the house and called everyone to attention.

"We've decided to investigate both murders with equal priority, given that they all but certainly had the same perpetrator," she told the gathering witches. "My associate will continue questioning everyone with regard to Coral Vervain's death, while I will begin a new investigation with a focus on Brenna Thorngrove's death."

"Wouldn't it save time if you left out the non-Head Witches?" Stephanie Underhill queried. "Both victims were murdered by someone who wields a sceptre."

"That doesn't mean they had no accomplices among the other attendees," Linda said. "Nobody can be discounted as a potential suspect."

Her gaze flicked over to me. I should have known she wouldn't dismiss my proximity to the crime scene, and I didn't know if she was aware that Brenna might have figured out the identity of Coral's killer and lost her life for it. If I was questioned first, then I'd tell her myself, but I didn't know how much sway my input would have when I was the one who'd found her body.

"That said," she added, "we would like to request that all the Head Witches hand their sceptres over to us for the duration of the investigation to prevent any more tragic deaths."

Exclamations of outrage arose from among the Head Witches, who began shouting at Linda. I backed away from the noise to find a quiet corner to wait in while I figured out what the hell to do next. It'd be nice if I knew where *my* familiar had disappeared to, but I wouldn't do myself any favours if I disobeyed Linda's order to stay within sight of the house.

"Hey." Robin's voice came from near my shoulder, and I jumped. "Sorry, didn't mean to startle you."

"It's okay." I turned towards her. "Did you already hand in your sceptre?"

"I did. The others aren't so keen on the idea." She pulled a face. "Did Rebecca's familiar ever show up?"

"No, but we didn't get to search the whole house." I gestured at the building. "Not that it's an easy place to search."

"I know, right?" she said. "It's like a funhouse without the 'fun' part."

I made a noncommittal noise in reply.

"I'll ask Tansy if she can sneak in and have a look around," she said. "It's time I got an update from her on whether she's heard anything from eavesdropping on the hunters outside."

"Good call." Out of any better ideas, I followed her around the garden until we spotted the bright-red tail of a squirrel. Tansy was perched on top of a fence and squeaked a greeting to both of us.

"Hey, Tansy," said Robin. "Find anything?"

Tansy let out a few squeaks and ran up and down the top of the fence before jumping onto Robin's shoulder.

"She said the hunters at the gates are mostly talking about shift changes and boring routine crap," Robin translated. "She also said that boyfriend of yours was with them."

My face heated. "Yeah. He's pretending to be friendly with them so he can learn if any of them are working with the enemy."

"You already told me that, remember?"

"I guess I did." I was mostly repeating the words to myself so I wouldn't forget that there was a reason Nathan was acting the way he was. Like I'd told Blythe, it wasn't anything personal. "Didn't they have anything to say about the murders?"

"What's that, Tansy?" She listened in as the squirrel squeaked a few times again. "She said the hunters were more interested in talking about what the murder might do to the reputation of the witches' council and the Head Witches. Nothing about who might be the culprit."

"They weren't talking about any prisoners at their high-security jail, then?"

Did that mean they weren't with Mrs Dailey? Or was one person working with her, and the others were unaware of that fact?

"Not that Tansy heard, sorry," she said. "She hasn't had time to eavesdrop on the hunters inside the house, though. Want her to go in there and look for your missing familiar while she's at it?"

"Sure," I said. "Thanks. I wish I could send *my* familiar to help out, but he's gone walkabout."

Her brows shot up. "Two familiars are missing?"

"Sky isn't missing. He's just... independent." Should I tell her he was a fairy cat? She must have heard of them, but I didn't need to complicate the situation even more by bringing up my own fairy heritage. "He's much smaller than Rebecca's cat, so he'd find it easy to hide. He's a little black cat with one white paw."

The squirrel squeaked again, and Robin nodded. "Tansy tells me she didn't see any cats near the gate, familiars or otherwise. She also didn't see who killed that Brenna Thorngrove, but you probably guessed that already."

I lowered my gaze. "Yeah. The last time I saw Brenna, she was hiding in the bushes near the crime scene. She wouldn't tell me why she was there, but I'm wondering if she figured something out that the rest of us didn't."

"Could be." Her expression turned preoccupied. "Who's your main suspect?"

"I don't have one. Do you?"

"Nope, but I hoped you did." Her gaze travelled over the other witches, who continued to shout ineffectually at the hunters as they carried armfuls of confiscated sceptres into the house.

At least the killer no longer held their main weapon, but who could it be? I also hadn't had time to talk to Nathalie Alder about her supposed visit to Mrs Dailey yet, but that might be unconnected to the deaths or just a show of opportunism from Rebecca and Blythe's scheming mother. As a non-Head Witch, she couldn't be the killer, at any rate.

Tansy squeaked, gesturing with a paw towards the witches' headquarters.

"Ready to go in?" I guessed. "I don't want you both to end up in trouble if she gets caught, though."

"She won't," said Robin. "With luck, she'll find your familiar *and* pin down which hunter we need to keep an eye on."

Tansy squeaked in agreement and then scurried away among the bushes, heading for the house. From that direction, Blythe stalked towards me—alone. Had they called Rebecca in for questioning about the second death already?

With my throat dry, I left Robin behind and approached Blythe. "Is Rebecca—?"

"Yes, she's going to talk to the hunters," she interrupted. "Turns out they've got it into their heads that the Head Witch who committed the murders might have been controlled against her will. And guess who's the only witch present with that kind of magic."

My heart dropped like a stone. "Rebecca."

10

I stared at Blythe, dread coursing through me despite the sheer absurdity of Rebecca being accused of mind controlling someone into committing murder. "Who came up with that one? How can they believe it?"

"I don't know," she said. "I'll ask my sister when they let her go, assuming they haven't already locked her up."

"They won't," I said, but the words felt hollow, and the hunters were unpredictable enough that I couldn't begin to guess what they'd do next.

I'd hoped that my being found at the scene of the second murder might take some of the heat off Rebecca if nothing else, but instead, they'd come up with a new way to blame her. She hadn't used her magic on another person in months, not since she'd learned to control it. But how could we possibly prove that?

Blythe narrowed her eyes. "Don't underestimate them."

"I thought one of them was working *with* her mother," I said in a low voice. "She wouldn't want Rebecca jailed, would she?"

Unless Mrs Dailey had thought the added threat would

make Rebecca desperate enough to agree to their deal after all, but why would the hunters take away Rebecca's only secure means of replying to her offer by capturing her familiar?

"They want someone to blame," Blythe said. "She's always been the obvious choice."

"Then it makes no sense for them to spring this on us now," I said. "Did they really not know about her abilities before Brenna's death?"

"I don't care when they found out. I care about my sister potentially being jailed," Blythe growled. "You can ask the hunters for the specifics if you like. I'm sure even you can't make things worse than they already are."

"Thanks for that," I muttered. "As a matter of fact, I want to know *who* they think Rebecca mind controlled into committing murder. She has her own sceptre, doesn't she? Why would she need to manipulate another Head Witch?"

"Do you really think they care about the logic?" she asked. "Don't you understand? The hunters have been paranoid ever since the Inquisitor was exposed as hiding his identity in plain sight. They don't want to admit to being fooled, so they need an obvious enemy to blame. Who better than the one person here capable of controlling someone against their will?"

My mouth fell open. I might have argued that the Inquisitor was a fairy and not a witch and had fooled them with illusions and not mind magic, but that didn't matter where the hunters were concerned.

Mrs Dailey herself hadn't needed to use magic to manipulate others, but it was from her that her children had inherited their powers. If I had to guess, I would say the hunters who didn't support Mrs Dailey saw her as their own personal bogeyman, the monster under the bed, and thought the same of her daughters, despite the towering evidence to the contrary.

"Until they have a clear idea as to which Head Witch Rebecca supposedly mind controlled, they'll have a hard job proving she did it," I said. "For one thing, wouldn't the Head Witch in question remember it all?"

"Again, they don't care for the technicalities. They'll twist anything if they can make it fit their narrative."

That, I could believe, but the irrationality of the explanation made no sense, and Blythe's understandable worries for her sister didn't make it any easier to figure out how many of her fears were justified. It'd help if I had another ally to offer a non-biased perspective, but with Nathan and Madame Grey keeping their distance and Robin having already told me everything she knew, who did that leave? Nobody I trusted enough to help me find the killer—that was for sure.

"And nobody's found her familiar yet?" I asked Blythe. "Ah... I don't suppose you've seen my familiar either?"

She gave me a scathing look. "I don't know why you're surprised that cat of yours has done a runner. He probably didn't trust you not to transport him into the middle of the lake."

That was uncalled for, but she turned about and stormed back towards the house before I could come up with a retaliation. *So much for Madame Grey insisting we work together.*

For now, I'd have to go it alone.

After checking nobody was within hearing distance, I whispered, "Sky, seriously, whatever you're doing can't be more important than this. I need your help."

No reply came.

"Sky," I hissed. "Sky, I'm not kidding. Toast is missing, and I—"

Someone cleared their throat behind me. I spun around to see Meredith Norwood several feet away from me. Heat rushed to my cheeks, though she wasn't the worst person who might have found me talking to someone who wasn't there, and I straightened upright.

"Sorry," she said. "Erm... who's Sky?"

"I was calling for my... my familiar." I was a terrible liar, and somehow even *that* sounded untruthful. "He has a tendency to wander off, but he's supposed to be here, and..."

"And you thought he might help you find Rebecca's familiar too?"

I stared at her for an instant before I remembered that word of Toast's disappearance would have reached everyone in the gardens by now. "Yes."

"I get it," she said. "I know it probably feels like you can't trust anyone, but I'm not going to rat you out to the hunters. I won't tell them a thing."

True, my lie-sensing power told me, but that didn't speak to her general trustworthiness.

"There's nothing to tell them," I blurted. "I mean, they already know Rebecca's familiar is missing, and they don't seem to care."

"Well, that's nice of them." She pursed her lips. "I don't have a familiar myself, but I bet they've never even had pets. The hunters don't seem like the type to care about animals any more than they care about people."

I made a noncommittal noise. Nathan did in fact have three cats, but he wasn't a hunter any longer, no matter how much he was currently acting like one. That was beside the point, anyway. "They won't let us search the house for him, and that's the only place we haven't looked yet."

"Ah." She studied my face. "You think he might be in trouble?"

"I don't know, but that house is a maze." While Meredith had professed to be on my side, that didn't mean I wanted her to know the leverage the hunters had over Rebecca, so I held my tongue on the subject. "Maybe it's nothing. He might have just fallen asleep in a spare room."

"I know you have no reason to trust me any more than any of the others," she said. "But two pairs of eyes are better than one, right? I can help you find him."

"I don't want you to get into trouble as well," I said. "The hunters seem pretty set on nobody wandering off, even if it's just to look for a missing familiar."

A gleam appeared in her eyes. "I don't mind causing a diversion. If I distract the hunters' attention, you can sneak into the house and search for your friend's familiar. How about that?"

Despite the ring of truth to her words, I hesitated. "Why would you do that?"

"I don't know. I just want to help out," she said. "I'm bored, too, and when I see a problem that needs solving, I'm inclined to want to help out. It's no big deal."

Hmm. Something about her offer wasn't quite right, but my lie-sensing power told me she'd told the truth so far. Maybe I was just being paranoid.

"Thanks," I said. "I appreciate the offer. Just... be careful not to get caught."

I might not be so lucky if I got myself lost in the house while searching for Toast and ended up getting caught. If it meant finding the identity of whoever was blackmailing Rebecca on her mother's behalf, though, I might have to risk it.

"Sure." She reached into her pocket for her wand.

"Haven't done this in a while, but I guess it's a good idea to get in some practise without my sceptre."

Oh. It'd slipped my mind that her sceptre was sealed in a downstairs room along with the others'. For most Head Witches, their magic was far amplified when they used the sceptre instead of a wand, but it was a little surprising that the hunters had let them retain access to at least one of their magical tools. Head Witches were generally accomplished enough that it didn't limit them to be without their sceptres, though a curse like the one that had killed Coral and Brenna might be less potent when cast using a wand.

As she turned towards the house, I reached into my pocket for my wand, debating for a moment whether to cast an unseen spell or use a glamour to hide myself instead. The former would invite fewer questions from Meredith, so I ducked behind a hedge to cast the spell that would render me unseen by anyone unless I walked directly in front of their faces.

A commotion arose from the direction of the house. Figuring that must be Meredith's distraction, I crossed the garden to the stone staircase in front of the house. The hunters guarding the doors had gone inside, drawn by whatever Meredith had done to snag their attention, but I kept to the shadows while I scanned the entrance hall to get my bearings.

Once again, the rooms seemed to have shuffled around, apparently without any of the hunters noticing or caring. As I approached the towering staircase in the centre, a potted plant went zooming past, followed by a valuable-looking vase, which zipped across the entrance hall as if it'd suddenly sprouted a pair of legs.

A crash echoed in the background, and I winced. Hoping this didn't end in disaster for Arabella Knotgrass's valuables, I seized the chance to climb the staircase to the upper floor while nobody was paying attention.

There, I found myself at the end of a long corridor—or rather, four corridors pointing at diagonal angles from the stairs and lined with doors that all appeared to be locked. This might get tricky, but as there was nobody upstairs but me, I had a little time to search—as long as the hunters were occupied with chasing runaway plant pots around, anyway.

"Toast?" I called out in a whisper. "Sky?"

A faint yowling sounded. I jumped, not having expected a reply. A second yowl prompted me to follow the noise to its source, one of the many closed doors leading to an office which presumably belonged to a member of the Knotgrass Coven. A piteous meowing noise that could only be Rebecca's familiar sounded when I tried to push it open then pulled the handle. The door held fast, locked and sealed with magical defences, no doubt. Someone clearly didn't want anyone breaking into their office, but who'd locked poor Toast in there in the first place?

I pulled out my wand and cast an unlocking charm with no result. The witch who'd owned this office must have put protections on the door, and I couldn't ask for Arabella Knotgrass's help without giving away that I was out of bounds.

Toast meowed again, a panicked noise that suggested he was afraid I'd run off and abandon him. I stayed put, trying all the variations of unlocking charm I'd learned, but none worked.

How had Toast got himself locked in there to begin with? If the door was already sealed, then it shouldn't have been possible for him to walk in without resistance. Even if someone had locked him in intentionally, they must have known how to undo the spell on the door to begin with—

which meant Arabella Knotgrass or someone connected to her coven had been responsible for shutting him in there.

A chill raced down my spine. I raised my wand, no longer feeling any particular guilt over the notion of damaging the Knotgrass Coven's property. My thoughts landed on one of the more dangerous spells Rita had taught Rebecca and me in the past few weeks—a conflagration charm—and I waved my wand.

The conflagration spell hit the wooden surface dead on, but instead of catching fire, the spell kind of melted off the door, sliding off its surface like a spilled potion on a wooden floor.

Weird. The shimmering effect on the wooden door didn't look like the average defensive shield. I was far from an expert, but... *Wait. It wasn't covered in an illusion spell, was it?*

I glanced behind me, inexplicably—if anyone caught me here, I'd be in trouble for far more than simply trying to open the door—and then lifted my right hand. My left hand was primarily for my witch magic, but my right was reserved for fairy magic, and through it, I felt for the strands of the illusion.

Sure enough, something snagged against my grip. I snapped my fingers, and the illusion unravelled, revealing a blank stretch of wall where there'd been a door only moments beforehand. The door was fake—but where had Toast's meowing come from?

"Toast?" I whispered again.

A yowl arose from behind a new door that'd appeared a few feet away, further down the wall. I trod in that direction, and this time when I tried an unlocking charm, the door sprang open.

A ball of orange fluff came zipping out of the room with the force of a bullet. Toast pelted towards the stairs, faster than I'd ever seen him move, while I hurried to catch up to him. When I reached the top of the stairs, I found myself looking down at several incredibly unimpressed hunters.

"What," one of them said, "are you doing up there?"

"Looking for Rebecca's familiar." I sheepishly descended the staircase to meet them. "Someone locked him in an upstairs room."

"You weren't supposed to be up there," said the hunter with the buzzed haircut.

"I heard him yowling from an upstairs window," I lied. "I knew he must be in the house, since I've looked everywhere outside. Sorry I went out of bounds."

A second hunter joined the first. "You're Blair Wilkes. You found the second victim, didn't you?"

"I found her body, but I didn't—"

The door to the questioning room flew open, and Rebecca ran out into the lobby, her expression frantic. "Toast?"

"Come back in here," Linda Graham demanded from inside the room. "At once."

"Sorry, it was my fault." I veered towards the room, conscious of the other hunters watching us both. "Rebecca's familiar went missing in the house, and he turned out to be locked in an upstairs room."

"Where is he now?" Rebecca asked me.

"I'll find him." I seized my chance to escape the hunters' accusing eyes. "He won't have gone far."

Not wanting to give anyone the chance to get their hands on her familiar again, I ran for the front door and nearly collided with Blythe at the top of the stairs. "Watch where you're going."

"I was looking for..." I saw her hands were covered with scratches. "Toast."

"He clawed me up when I grabbed him and ran off. What did you do to him?"

"What did *I* do?" I echoed. "I found him locked in an upstairs room. He flew at me as soon as I opened the door. Which was sealed with a magical illusion spell, by the way."

"It was *what*?" She swore under her breath. "Have you been breaking into Arabella's rooms on top of everything else?"

"Arabella, or someone who knows how her house's magic works, was responsible for locking him in that room, Blythe," I told her. "From now on, one of us has to watch him at all times."

On my way down the stone staircase, I caught sight of Meredith. She shot me an apologetic look, presumably because she hadn't intended for me to get caught, though it wasn't really her fault I'd drawn attention.

"Hey." I caught up to her near a flower bed. "Did you see him? Toast, I mean."

"I did, but he moved fast."

I scanned the area and spotted a familiar fluffy tail poking out from under a hedge. Crouching down, I reached out a hand.

"Toast, it's okay," I said soothingly. "Come on out."

Hesitantly, Toast wriggled out from underneath the flower bed and flopped into my arms. I could just imagine how Blythe would react, given that he'd clawed her up, but he was back to his usual placidity as I stroked his fluffy head.

"I don't suppose you've seen Sky?" I asked him conversationally. "I guess not, because he'd have been able to get you both out of that room easily enough. I wish I knew where he was."

Toast didn't make a sound. His entire body was trembling.

"Toast," I whispered. "Who locked you in that room? Was it one of the witches?"

He meowed plaintively. I didn't have the ability to understand him the way Robin did, but he could still communicate with Rebecca to some degree, and once she got out of questioning, she might be able to convince him to point to the culprit.

Only a witch could have set up that illusion spell, but it might have already been on the door before any of us had arrived here. The only way to know for sure would be to ask the house's owner, but Arabella wouldn't take kindly to being accused of attacking Rebecca's familiar, let alone the mess Meredith's diversion had made of the lower floor.

I lifted Toast with the intention of carrying him closer to the other witches, but he meowed loudly and jumped out of my arms, wriggling underneath the nearest flower bed.

"Toast." I reached for him. "Rebecca will be out of questioning soon. You'll be able to see her."

Toast meowed, a quiet, scared sound. Then I saw Meredith striding toward us, her expression urgent.

"Sorry, Blair," she said. "Ah, I heard the hunters talking, and... well, it sounds like Rebecca has been officially labelled as the main suspect for the murders."

11

─────────

"What was the point in questioning everyone else if they always planned to accuse her?" I burst out, my thoughts in disarray. *They can't blame Rebecca. It's absurd.*

"I know," Meredith said. "The hunters care more about their reputations than actually finding the real culprit. That's nothing new."

I hadn't known she had personal experience with the hunters, though her comments about Mrs Dailey made more sense in that light. "Yeah, but they could have picked literally anyone else and had a stronger case. Rebecca isn't the killer."

"I don't know that they'll listen to you," she said. "They seem to respect that Madame Grey, though, right?"

"Right. I have to find her." I didn't know what else to do.

"I'll watch Rebecca's familiar," Meredith offered. "If he ever comes out of there."

"All right. Thanks." I didn't want to leave him again, but at least he'd hidden in a public place this time, so if he ran off, someone would spot him.

In the meantime, I went in search of Madame Grey. The front doors were unguarded, and upon entering, I found Blythe arguing with the hunter outside the questioning room.

"You can't name my sister as the prime suspect," she insisted. "She's a minor, and she didn't murder either of those people. If she supposedly mind controlled someone, then why hasn't anyone else come forward?"

"If the person in question was unaware of being controlled, then they'd be unable to confess," said the hunter. "Especially if they're dead."

"Who's dead?" I asked blankly.

Blythe levelled a glare at me. "They've got it into their heads that my sister made *Brenna* kill Coral Vervain."

"Your sister wasn't able to adequately deny these accusations."

"You think she controlled *Brenna*?" Honestly, they'd lost their collective minds. "Then who's supposed to have killed Brenna? She can't have murdered herself."

"We're still gathering information from the other Head Witches," said the hunter. "Rebecca will remain in custody until then."

"But—" Anger churned inside me. "Can you at least let her see her familiar? He's currently hiding under a bush after being locked in an upstairs room behind a magically sealed door, which nobody has been able to explain."

"He probably locked himself in," the hunter said dismissively. "And you shouldn't have been up there to begin with, Blair Wilkes."

I opened my mouth to argue and closed it. After all, I couldn't tell them that someone had given Toast a note from Mrs Dailey without getting us both into even more trouble than we were already in. I'd forgotten I needed to talk to

Arabella about that door, but compared to Rebecca's imminent arrest, it all seemed trivial. And where was Madame Grey?

The guard stepped aside when Linda Graham exited the questioning room, looking between Blythe and me. "You're the ones causing a disturbance, are you?"

Blythe flushed bright red. "This isn't justice. You're just blaming my sister because it's convenient. There's zero proof she used her magic at all."

"There's also no proof she didn't, by the same logic," Linda said. "She's done it before."

"By *accident*!" Blythe exploded, having apparently found her spine. "There isn't a single good reason for her to want Coral *or* Brenna dead."

"They were rivals to power who challenged her legitimacy to the title of Head Witch. Isn't that enough?"

"No." Blythe stepped forward. "Absolutely not. You're supposed to be here as impartial judges, but you aren't acting like it at all."

"On the contrary, we are doing exactly what we were asked to do, despite the adverse circumstances." She gave me a brief dismissive look. "Now both of you leave, before I have you confined as well as your sister."

"C'mon." I caught Blythe's arm and all but dragged her away from the hunters to the back door. "Let's find Rebecca's familiar and bring him to her. She needs him."

She twisted out of my reach. "You're giving up?"

"Of course I'm not, but they aren't going to let your sister go if you lose your temper with them, are they?" I let go of her arm, and she reluctantly followed me outside.

"Where's that cat?" Blythe growled, scanning the garden.

"Hiding under a flower bed, the last I saw." I moved in

that direction. "I was going to find Robin and ask her to confirm who gave him that letter. Where is she?"

"Who cares?"

"She can understand animals, Blythe," I pointed out. "Robin can ask Toast who locked him in that room as well."

"That doesn't matter either."

"Don't be absurd." Now who was giving up? "Any information we can get that might take the attention off your sister is worth pursuing. Besides, the way they came to their decision makes no sense, unless they're answering to someone outside. Rebecca being arrested plays right into your mother's hands. This is her doing. I'm sure."

"Then what're you actually going to do about it, genius?"

"I..." I hadn't got that far yet. "Expose the hunters who are working with her, for a start. They'll have a harder job justifying their authority if it gets out that some of them are in league with a criminal."

"That's not enough," she said. "It certainly won't stop them arresting my sister, and it won't help us find the real killer either."

"Neither will arguing with the hunters." I made for the flower bed where Toast had been hiding under Meredith's watchful eye.

"Hey," she said. "Is everything okay?"

"Not really." There was no point in being anything other than honest, not when she already knew about the murder accusation.

"Sorry, I guess that wasn't the right question," she said. "Though if she's been arrested, then I hope she'll get a trial and a chance to explain herself at the very least. Right?"

"Huh?" I frowned. "No, they haven't arrested her yet. They're going to put her under watch while they question the other Head Witches."

"Oh." She paused for a moment as if thinking over her words. "That's good. I mean, it might mean they're giving others the chance to expose more information."

"What are you doing here?" Blythe asked from behind me. "Go away. We don't need to hear your opinions on this. It's none of your business."

"Blythe," I said. "That's enough."

"I guess you're right." Meredith backed away from the flower bed. "I'm sorry about your sister."

"Wait." Ignoring Blythe, I went in pursuit of Meredith. "Please don't pay any attention to her."

"She's worried about her sister. I get it," she said with a forced smile. "It's no problem."

"Have you seen Robin?" I asked her.

"Robin?" she echoed. "No. I haven't. Sorry."

Thanks, Blythe. She might have a very good reason to be upset, but that didn't mean she had to alienate our few potential allies. I didn't need her to do the same with Robin, so I left her to coax poor Toast out from behind the flower bed and approached the other witches. Robin wasn't with them, but when Arabella Knotgrass scowled in my direction, I remembered my resolution to find out just how Rebecca's familiar had ended up locked in that office to begin with.

I approached Arabella, trying to ignore her hostile expression. "Excuse me. Can I talk to you for a second?"

"What?" she growled. "Were you the one who broke my vase?"

Oops. I didn't want to tell tales on Meredith, so I said, "No, but I found Rebecca's familiar locked in an upstairs office, and I wondered who put those security spells on the door."

She straightened upright. "You've been breaking into my offices too?"

"No, I…" Well, I kind of had. "I didn't mean to, but he was panicking, and I couldn't figure out whose office it was."

She puffed up in outrage. "That's no excuse. Make no mistake, I'll be reporting this at once."

Before I could say another word, she stormed off in the direction of the house, leaving me wondering who she intended to report *to*. She didn't see the hunters as the authority, did she?

"What did you do to her?" asked one of the witches, looking intrigued.

"Someone locked Rebecca's familiar in an upstairs office," I explained. "Arabella was upset with me for letting him out and undoing the security spells on the door in the process."

"Oh, that explains it," she said, chuckling. "She'll have it in for you now."

"It's not funny," I said, annoyed. "He didn't lock himself in there, so she can blame the person who did. Is Arabella the only person with control over the house's magic?"

"No, of course not," said the witch. "Her whole coven is. Really, do you have no sense of humour?"

"Oh, I expect she's upset that her friend's been arrested," Jodie Atwater said, overhearing. "Personally, I'm not surprised. Like mother, like daughter."

I spun on her. "She's nothing like her mother. In fact, if anyone here *is* likely to have been involved in these murders, it's Mrs Dailey's former allies. Anyone want to confess?"

All the witches in the vicinity gaped at me. This wasn't entirely how I'd planned to tease out which people present had once been allied with Rebecca's mother, but it was clear that dancing around the subject would get me nowhere.

Jodie Atwater gave a laugh. "Allies? Your friend Rebecca did her mother's bidding for years."

"Under duress," I said, my temper spiking anew. "The hunters have no idea who the killer is. They're blaming Rebecca because it's convenient and a reason not to admit to their own incompetence."

"Ah, but she was found at the crime scene, wasn't she?" asked Jodie. "And *you* were found at the other, Blair."

"Whatever happened to innocent until proven guilty?" I understood why Blythe had lost her temper altogether. "I know that's not the hunters' mantra, but they shouldn't even be here."

"They're not perfect, but they're decisive and thorough," said Catherine Oakley. "Exactly what we need at the moment."

"If the hunters make the wrong decision, it's as bad as not making one at all," I argued. "Would you say the same if you were the one they set up to take the fall?"

"Who is 'they'?" Catherine arched a delicate brow. "You mean the hunters?"

"I was referring to whoever is behind the murders." Did it really matter if everyone knew I suspected the hunters themselves of being involved in setting up Rebecca, though?

From the way Catherine Oakley's face flushed, she'd guessed my meaning. "You should know that the hunters are committed and trained to be impartial."

"Impartial?" She had to be joking. "Even if you ignore the fact that they'd be happy to see every one of you stripped of your power, Rebecca isn't the killer, and it's irresponsible and disrespectful to the victims for the hunters to pretend otherwise."

I turned away, seething, before she could argue any further. I didn't truly think all the hunters were on the side of the killer, but at least one of them was allied with Mrs Dailey, and wasn't that the same thing?

As for the witches? I watched Nathalie out of the corner of my eye while I waited for the other witches to return to their previous conversations. I'd all but run out of ideas on how to coax answers from her, but one approach remained —honesty.

When I was certain nobody else was watching us, I strode over to Nathalie's side. "I need to talk to you alone."

"We're not supposed to wander off" came her reply.

"I'm aware, but trust me, you don't want this to be overheard."

After several moments of silence, she exhaled a sigh. Then, as if resigned, she followed me a short distance towards the fountain, where the splashing noise would make it harder for us to be overheard.

"Well?" she said.

"I wanted to talk to you about... about Mrs Dailey."

She raised a brow, a faint flush spreading across her cheeks, but she said nothing.

"You visited her in jail recently," I went on. "Didn't you?"

"Would you really expect me to tell *you* that?"

"I already know because I have someone who keeps tabs on her." Technically, Blythe had the contact, not me, but she didn't need to know the details. "You're the only person I know who's recently spoken to her, unless you can point me to her other former allies."

"I'm not her former ally," she said. "Yes, I voted for her proposals when she was on the regional witch council, as did so many others, including half the witches present here. It doesn't prove a thing."

True.

"Then why did you visit her in jail?"

"Why does that matter?"

"Because," I said carefully, with a swooping sensation inside, as though my feet teetered at the edge of a cliff, "she made contact with me too. Specifically, she made me an offer. If something similar happened to you, I wondered how you handled it."

She stared at me for an instant. "That depends on your priorities, but I'm not the person to ask."

"You mean you said no?" I surmised. "I'm not going to tell tales to the hunters, you know."

"If she made contact with you at all, then you're in trouble," she said. "I only agreed to visit her because she claimed to be able to solve my coven's financial problems, but it was obvious when I spoke to her directly that she was lying."

"She shouldn't be able to solve anything from behind bars." I frowned. "She has allies in the outside world, sure, but who exactly does she have delivering messages for her? Nobody seems to know, but it seems a massive oversight on behalf of her jailors."

"I have no idea," she said. "I found the letter outside my office, with no name attached. If anyone else received the same, then they certainly haven't mentioned it to me."

"How recently?" Had she been offered more freedom than any of us had known? "When did she contact you?"

"A few weeks ago," she murmured with a glance over at the house. "I hope you aren't planning to tell that friend of yours. Her daughter."

"Her daughter is being blamed for two murders she didn't commit." If she didn't already know, then she would soon. "Her mother terrorised her for years. How can any of you have supported someone like that?"

"Are you truly that naïve?" she asked quietly. "Mrs

Dailey's personal life was a secret from all but her closest advisors, but I shouldn't have to justify myself to the likes of you, Blair Wilkes."

Okay. Maybe that was too much. I held up my hands. "I'm not judging you. I'm trying to understand."

"I don't need to have your lie-sensing power to know that isn't true," she said in sharp tones. "Do you think you're special for resisting her? You don't know the first thing about why so many of us voted for her reforms to the coven system. We spent years if not decades ignored by our own covens and by the Head Witches as a collective. That left us with little choice but to turn to someone who seemed to understand our needs."

"When you visited her in jail, you changed your mind, though," I said. "Why was that?"

"With her resources stripped away, I saw her for what she truly was." She drew in a breath. "Whatever she wants, don't give it to her, Blair. It's not worth it."

12

Nathalie's words lurked in the back of my mind as I walked away from her. *It's not worth it.* But what was Rebecca's freedom worth? What if the only way to help her was to contact Mrs Dailey?

That might be exactly what Mrs Dailey wanted us to think, of course, and I couldn't entirely rely on Nathalie's perspective either. She hadn't lied, but she might easily have omitted information about her visit to the jail or her reasons for replying to her offer at all. There was no guarantee the others hadn't visited her for less-than-benign reasons, without Blythe knowing, but I had zero desire to make myself into a target for her anger by asking.

The only person who had the full story was Mrs Dailey herself, and I certainly didn't want to talk to *her*, even from the other side of the door to her cell—even if she was Rebecca's only hope for freedom, which was doubtful, since not all the hunters here were on her side. Nathan, for one, would have noticed if they were. *Wouldn't he?*

Doubts filled my mind, as persistent as the bees hovering over the flower beds, while I circled the garden and tried not to think about what Rebecca might be enduring inside the house. I almost hoped the hunters would find someone else to blame instead, guilty or not, but their target had always been her.

If Linda Graham wasn't allied with Mrs Dailey, though, I had to wonder how she'd managed to convince herself that Rebecca had mind controlled two other Head Witches into committing murder. How could nobody else see how irrational her accusations were? You'd think the other Head Witches would not be impressed with the insinuation that their formidable magic was no match for an eleven-year-old with limited training.

And just where was Robin? If she was being questioned, she should really have returned by now, but there was no sign of her in the garden. When I spotted her mother near a fountain, I made my way over.

"Excuse me, have you seen Robin?" I asked her.

"She went looking for that familiar of hers," she replied.

"Looking for her?" I echoed. "Why? Tansy's not missing, is she?"

"Her familiar likes to wander off." She sniffed. "She's flighty, and Robin gives her far too much freedom."

Despite her dismissive tone, her words triggered another spike of nerves. "Er, not to worry you, but Rebecca's familiar went missing earlier and turned out to be locked in a magically sealed upstairs office."

She blinked. "What did she do that for?"

"She didn't," I said. "I mean, I don't actually know who locked her cat in there, but Rebecca hasn't even set foot upstairs. It wasn't her."

Lady Wildwood didn't appear concerned, but I couldn't make her take this any more seriously without admitting to her daughter's plan to spy on the hunters. Lady Wildwood was the definition of rule-following and would no doubt disapprove of Robin's actions. Moreover, we couldn't guarantee that she wouldn't tell any of the other witches present the truth... including the killer.

All the same, a law-abiding coven leader like her wouldn't be impressed at the notion of the wrong person being arrested, right?

"I assume he's safe now," she said. "I wouldn't worry about my daughter or her wayward familiar, but I'll look for her. She won't have gone far."

No doubt Robin wouldn't be thrilled if I brought her mother after her, so I hastened to distract her. "No, I'm sure she won't have, but I did have a question. Do you know if anyone other than Arabella's coven has the ability to control the magic on her house?"

She raised her brows at my abrupt change of topic. "The Knotgrass Coven alone has control over the house's magic, yes. It's a touch excessive, in my view, but it enables Arabella to feel important. Is there a reason you wanted to know?"

Wow, that was cold. "I wanted to know because Rebecca's familiar went missing and turned out to be locked in an upstairs room. Someone who knows the house's magic locked him in there, but... the thing is, it might be because he heard something he shouldn't have, and if he'd told Robin, she'd have been able to understand him." The last part came out in a blurt, not at all helped by her expression of polite incredulity.

"What exactly does that mean?" she enquired. "Is this to do with whatever you and my daughter were scheming together?"

Oops. "I wouldn't use the word 'scheming,' but my own coven leader did ask me to talk to as many people as possible to see if we could narrow down the identity of the killer." I didn't have anything to lose by telling her that. "I know the hunters are supposed to be in charge of the questioning, but I don't think they're acting in good faith. I can tell when people are lying, and Robin can understand animals, so we hoped..."

"You hoped you'd be the ones to solve the crime. I know. It's just like my daughter. She has yet to grasp the notion that it's unbecoming for a Head Witch to interfere in concerns that aren't her own."

That seemed more than a little unfair. "It's hardly interfering if her familiar overhears important information, is it? In fact, the last time I spoke to her, she said that Tansy heard the hunters talking about the power they might be able to leverage over the Head Witches as a result of the murders. And now... and now it looks like both of them have disappeared.

"So I see." Her nostrils flared. "I doubt she's run into any trouble, but if Robin is somewhere she isn't supposed to be, then I'll ensure she doesn't do any further damage."

"Damage?" When she strode away, I hurried after her, mildly alarmed. "She's not doing anything wrong by *talking* to people."

Lady Wildwood ignored me, quickening her pace. We were way out of the part of the garden the hunters had confined us to, but she kept walking until we veered around a corner and came into view of the back gate on the other side of the house.

There, far from being missing, Robin stood with Tansy perched on her shoulder and her back to us.

"You're breaking the rules," she was saying to the hunters guarding the back gates. "Not just of the Head Witch rulebook but of your own organisation too. There's no authorisation for you to arrest people based on nothing but conjecture."

"And what qualifies you to speak on the subject?" To my horror, none other than Linda Graham responded. Wasn't she supposed to be inside the house? "You're Robin Wildwood, aren't you? From what I hear, you only attained your position because you won out in a family feud and had no prior experience of leadership."

Robin's shoulders tensed. "My brother's the head of my local police force. I know more than a little about the laws of the paranormal world, believe it or not."

"Robin!" said Lady Wildwood. "Mrs Graham, I'm sorry. I know she shouldn't be out here."

Linda Graham gave her an appraising look. "At least one of you has manners."

Robin's face flushed. "As if manners matter more than the laws. Are you still trying to arrest people who haven't committed any crimes?"

"Nobody has been arrested," Linda said, "but Rebecca Dailey has implicated herself in both murders by the very nature of her magical talents."

"That's absurd," I said before I could think better of it. "It'd be like assuming I was totally virtuous because I can tell truth from lie. Magical talents are something we're born with. They have no bearing on our actual behaviour."

"Exactly," Robin said. "Also, Tansy overheard several of your hunters talking about how they plan to undermine the witch councils by using Rebecca's arrest as proof the Head Witches are corrupt. There's nothing in their plans that involves finding the actual criminal. In fact, if a non-Head Witch turns out to be the culprit, they lose all authority and have to slink back to their base in disgrace. It was more worth their while to blame one of us."

"Seriously?" That would explain a lot, and Rebecca had always been the most obvious target.

"That's enough, Robin," said Lady Wildwood. "Like it or not, the hunters were appointed to find the killer, and it's inappropriate for you to challenge them."

"They appointed themselves, mother." Robin took a step back when Lady Wildwood tried to grab her arm. "Speaking of not appropriate, you're forgetting who the Head Witch is here."

Her tone sounded as if she wished it were otherwise. She might outrank Lady Wildwood, but I could tell she wasn't used to being the one with superior status, and neither was her mother. Letting her daughter's arm drop, Lady Wildwood turned away—and that was when I spotted a second group of hunters approaching, including Nathan.

Had he overheard any of our confrontation? I didn't know, but as painful as it was to turn my back on him, he'd already made it clear that I couldn't talk to him when the other hunters were around. And I definitely couldn't get away with making accusations against the others.

Robin gave the hunters one last glare and followed her mother around the path circling the house, while I hurried to catch up to her. "Robin, I believe you. What did Tansy overhear?"

"The same as usual." She made a disgruntled noise. "That Linda Graham must have read the Head Witch's rule-book inside and out, because her group of minions took advantage of every loophole in there. The only way for them to outrank the Head Witches and have any authority at all is if they believe one of us is unquestionably guilty, and since they couldn't find any dirt on the others..."

"Only because they weren't looking for it." Anger clenched my fists. "The theory they've come up with is even more ridiculous than the idea of Rebecca committing murder. Instead, they've got it into their heads that she mind controlled someone else into doing it."

Robin halted in her steps. "Rebecca can mind control people? Really?"

"It's not mind control, it's more... more of a subtle influence over their personalities." I stumbled over the words in an effort to make her understand. "If she'd used it on anyone here, we'd know—and I'm not sure if it would even work on another Head Witch in the first place."

"Not much of an argument on the hunters' behalf, then."

"Linda seems to take it pretty seriously." I sucked in a breath. "One of the other hunters even suggested Rebecca forced Brenna to murder Coral, but that leaves the question of who killed Brenna herself. Linda's argument is full of holes, but nobody else among the hunters seems to care."

Tansy squeaked loudly, and Robin's brows shot up. "I'd translate that, but it's not appropriate for polite company. Also, for the record, that's underhanded of her. Linda, I mean."

"Tell me about it." I heaved a sigh. "I couldn't even find out who locked the upstairs room. That reminds me—we found Rebecca's familiar."

"You found him?"

"He was locked in someone's office on the upstairs floor of the house." We rounded the corner into the main part of the garden. "Last I saw, he was hiding under a flower bed, but maybe he'll talk to you."

The slight problem was neither Toast nor Blythe was anywhere to be seen, and the only person standing near the flower bed was Meredith Norwood.

"Looking for that pleasant friend of yours?" Meredith

asked. "She took the cat with her and went back into the house. I thought you'd want to know."

True... and also a lie. Which part, though? "I didn't think anyone was allowed in."

She shrugged. "I guess she got fed up with not knowing what was going on in there."

That sounded like Blythe, but had she forgotten we needed to find out both who'd given Toast the note from Mrs Dailey and who'd locked him in the house? If her anger with the hunters had overtaken her reasoning, then she might need a reminder. Leaving Robin and Meredith behind, I made for the stairs to the house, only to find my path barred by two hunters.

"You again?" asked the hunter with the shaved head. "I take it you're the one Arabella has been complaining about?"

"Huh?" *Oh, great. She's been telling tales on me.* "If you mean to ask if I'm the one who found Rebecca's familiar locked in one of her offices, then yes. Have you seen him? Or Blythe?"

"No more funny business from you," said the hunter. "You're staying outside, where we can see you."

"I'm not—I only wanted to know where she is," I said. "I wasn't trying to make trouble earlier. Someone locked Rebecca's familiar in a magically secured office, and all I did was let him out."

"I'm not interested in your petty squabbles," said the hunter. "Go on. Hop it."

"I need to talk to Rebecca."

"I'll pass on the message."

Lie. As I'd expected, but when I felt the distinct sense of being watched, I glanced behind me. At the foot of the stairs, Arabella glowered at me from near the other witches.

If I had to guess, I would say she was busy bad-mouthing me for breaking into her offices. *Great.*

Robin stood apart from the other witches, so I descended and joined her. "They won't let me in."

"Well, that's inconvenient," she said. "What did you do earlier? I heard something about runaway plant pots."

"That was Meredith," I explained. "She offered to create a diversion so I could search for Rebecca's familiar inside the house. Arabella flipped out at me when I asked who locked him in the office, because I had to undo her security spells to get him out."

She wrinkled her nose. "Where's he gone now, then? The cat, I mean."

"Blythe took him... somewhere." I looked up at the house's many windows, but it was beyond me to tell her location. "The guards wouldn't tell me where they went."

"Then we'll ask the others." Robin approached the nearest group of witches, all of whom looked down their noses at us. "Hey, have you seen Blythe, Rebecca's sister? She was with that orange cat."

"I expect she's gone to fight for her sister." Stephanie Underhill wore a barely concealed smirk that I had little doubt was due to Rebecca's predicament.

Anger stirred inside me. "I just want to know where she is. Have any of you seen her?"

Another witch answered, "She went into the house. Talked her way past those hunters."

"Which hunters?"

"I don't know. They all look the same to me."

She might have meant the ones at the doors, but a chill raced over my skin. While Blythe might have gone to argue against her sister's arrest, the timing made me suspicious, and I found myself pacing back to the flower bed where

Toast had been hiding. *Why take him with her? She knows he might have information we need.*

Robin caught me up, Tansy clinging to her shoulder. "She might be talking to them about her sister. I don't blame her for taking the cat with her too."

"I told her that you'd be able to understand him." Worry fluttered inside me. "I know she isn't listening to me at the moment, but I can't find the real killer without her cooperation."

Robin lowered her gaze, while Tansy gave a despondent squeak. "I'm sorry. I wish I could be of more help. Are there any other former allies of Mrs Dailey here? Do you know?"

I drew in a breath. "Nathalie Alder was the last person who visited Mrs Dailey in jail, but she claimed to have turned down her offer. It sounds like she's been blackmailing other people from behind bars, not just us, but Nathalie insisted that she had nothing to do with Rebecca being accused, and neither did any of her other former allies."

"I suppose you'd know if she was lying," said Robin. "Then... who else is left?"

"Arabella... she wasn't happy about my breaking into the upstairs office, so maybe she's the one who locked Toast in there." That didn't give me much to go on, though. "Or she's just angry about the intrusion. I have no idea."

"Hey..." Robin sucked in a breath, crouching down. "Check this out."

I dropped to her level and saw a piece of paper lying in the flower bed. I scooped it up, my pulse racing.

I heard your freedom hangs by a thread, the note read. *If you've changed your mind and want to request my help, a simple yes will do. If not, I'll assume you've accepted your fate. I look forward to seeing you soon.*

The note was for Rebecca, but she wasn't here to answer. Had Blythe seen who'd left the note? Was that where she'd disappeared to?

Whatever the case, the message was as clear as day. If one of us didn't leave a reply, Rebecca would be at risk of losing her freedom without having ever done anything wrong.

"If that's directed at Rebecca," said Robin, her voice barely a whisper, "she can hardly leave a reply when she's in custody, can she? Someone didn't think this through."

"No." I turned the note over to see if it said anything else, and the paper fell apart in my hands. Grains of dust slipped between my fingers along with our only proof of the hunters' treachery. "I... I don't think it means they didn't think it through."

If Rebecca couldn't reply, then there was one person left who could—me.

13

———

I stared into the flower bed, as if another note would appear with an explanation if I looked hard enough. Did Mrs Dailey know her daughter had been taken into custody? Not if she assumed she was freely able to reply to her note, unless she'd expected Blythe to reply in her stead. *Where is she, though?*

"They took her," I murmured. "The hunters took Blythe."

Robin didn't answer. She didn't need to. We both knew the hunters had been set on abusing their authority from the start, but kidnapping someone in plain sight was a step too far. The question was, *which* hunters had taken her? Had Blythe refused her mother's offer, or had she never seen the note at all? If the latter, was Mrs Dailey's ally still lurking around, waiting for a response?

"I can't let this stand." I reached into my pockets in search of something to write on and unearthed a crumpled receipt. "Ah, do you have a pen I can borrow?"

"You're not going to reply." Robin reached into her pocket. "Are you?"

"I am," I said. "I'm not accepting the offer, though. I just want to know what she'll say when it's me who replies and not Rebecca."

Mrs Dailey had tried to have *me* arrested more than once, so this wasn't likely to end in my favour either, but Rebecca couldn't reply, and neither could her sister.

"Or how she delivers the reply," added Robin. "I wonder if we can catch her ally in the act."

"Good point." When Robin handed me a pen, I straightened out the receipt and scribbled a reply.

R is in custody. It's just me now. Does the offer still stand?

I debated signing off using my initials or another clue to indicate who was responding, but it was too risky. I doubted any of the witches would go poking around the flower bed unless they knew what they might find in there, but the hunters were another story. I dropped the note while Robin exchanged a few words with Tansy.

"Tansy is going to hide under the flower bed and follow whoever picks up your note," she said. "That okay?"

"Sure, but be careful." I addressed the last part to the little red squirrel, who squeaked in understanding. "They already locked poor Toast in that upstairs room, so I don't think they're above hurting people's familiars to get their way."

Now he *and* Blythe were missing, and for all I knew, they weren't even on the property any longer. The hunters who'd taken them had left no traces behind.

"Don't worry about us," Robin said. "I doubt the hunters have ever dealt with a familiar like Tansy before."

The little squirrel squeaked in agreement and darted underneath the flower bed, while I gave Robin her pen back. Now all we had to do was act as normal as possible while the hunters took the reply straight to Mrs Dailey.

It would make me look less suspicious if I kept my distance from Robin, but since none of the other witches would speak to me, I was left to pace in circles and wonder whether I shouldn't have come up with a better plan. Even Mrs Dailey didn't seem to know that her daughter had been arrested as the main suspect, which suggested the hunters hadn't been keeping her apprised of the situation, and even if she did reply to my note, there was no guarantee that her offer would arrive in time to spare Rebecca from arrest or worse.

With Blythe gone, Rebecca was almost out of allies... with one exception. Madame Grey wasn't among the other witches in the garden, so she could only be inside the house, arguing for Rebecca's freedom. She didn't need to be burdened with the knowledge that Mrs Dailey had given her daughter an ultimatum, but what if the very hunters who held Rebecca's freedom in their hands were also her mother's messengers?

Fighting back a tidal wave of despair mingled with panic, I climbed the staircase yet again and approached the hunters guarding the front doors to the house.

"Where is Madame Grey?" I asked them. "I need to talk to her. Urgently."

"We've heard enough from you, Blair Wilkes," said the same guy who'd barred my way beforehand. "You're trying to distract us in the hopes of freeing your friend, aren't you?"

"She's innocent, but that's beside the point," I said. "I need to talk to Madame Grey about something unrelated but equally urgent."

"We'd be happy to pass on the message."

I didn't need to be able to sense lies to know he had zero intention of doing so. "I have to talk to her face to face. Can you let her know that? *She* isn't in custody."

"Looking for an excuse to sneak into the house and cause trouble again?" he asked. "I don't think so. You've done nothing but try to disrupt our investigation from the start, Blair Wilkes."

This hardly counts as an investigation. You decided Rebecca was guilty before you got here. "That's untrue. The only disruption I caused was when I set Rebecca's familiar free from the room someone locked her in. All I'm asking is for the chance to talk to my coven leader."

"It's not our problem if she doesn't want to talk to you," said the second hunter. "Sensible, if you ask me."

My hands fisted. "She outranks *your* authority, if you've forgotten, even now."

I hadn't intended my mouth to get the better of me, but the hunters' smugness was almost too much to bear. They already thought they'd won.

The hunter looked down at me. "Are you volunteering to be the next to be questioned?"

"I didn't realise you *were* still questioning people." If it got me into the house and close to Madame Grey, I'd take any risk necessary. "I thought you'd already made up your minds."

"I think this one should have a word with Linda," said the first hunter. "See if it knocks her attitude down a peg."

A surge of recklessness seized me. "I'm not the one whose attitude needs looking at. This isn't even your house, and you know nothing about the witches you're trying to replace."

"Again, you're only proving you don't understand the situation, Blair," said the hunter. "Come on. I'll take you to Linda in person."

I'd pretty much asked for it, so I let him escort me into

the entrance hall. While the rooms had shifted again, one of the interrogation rooms was now empty.

"You haven't already finished questioning everyone about Coral's death, have you?" I hadn't expected to be questioned myself, given that I hadn't been on the property at the time, but they hadn't told the rest of us if they'd come to any conclusions.

"We have," the hunter replied. "All the evidence suggests that Coral Vervain was killed by Brenna Thorngrove while she was under the influence of another witch's magic."

"You mean that's what Linda says," I said heatedly. "She's basing that on no evidence whatsoever except an irrational hatred of Rebecca and her magic. Has she decided who supposedly killed Brenna herself yet, or is she still waiting to find another person to blame?"

Madame Grey's voice drifted from the direction of the council meeting room. I veered that way, but the hunter grabbed my arm. "Not so fast. We're going to talk to Linda."

"Let go of me." I struggled to escape his grip, but when we reached the interrogation room, the door opened, and Linda herself emerged. "What is going on?"

"Blair has generously volunteered to be questioned next," he said.

I glared at him then at Linda. "I requested to talk to my coven leader. This was apparently the only way to get into the building."

She arched a brow. "Meredith, you can leave. Blair, you'll have your wish."

Meredith left the room—giving me a brief look of sympathy—before the hunter holding my arm unceremoniously shoved me through the open door.

When Linda Graham and I were alone together, she said, "I have to admit I hoped you'd be more understanding of your friend's predicament, Blair. If you've come to confess in her place, it won't work."

"What?" Her directness threw me for a loop, and it disarmed me that she could sound so rational despite the bizarre nonsense coming out of her mouth. Did she really believe her own words so thoroughly?

"To business," she said. "You found Brenna's body, didn't you?"

"Yes," I said. "Earlier, I found her searching the bushes near the scene of Coral Vervain's death. I believe she figured out who killed Coral and was ambushed by the killer before she could tell anyone."

"Really, now," she said. "And do you have any ideas as to the identity of the killer?"

Is she not committed to arresting Rebecca after all? Or does she just want to see what I say? "Not Rebecca. She had no opportunity to be alone with Brenna in the minutes before her death. She was either with me or with Blythe the whole time."

"Rebecca's sister," she said. "Yes, I hoped to talk to her as well. I'm surprised she wasn't as willing to fight on her behalf as I expected."

"You haven't?" I frowned. "I thought she came into the house not long ago along with Rebecca's familiar."

"That's incorrect. I certainly haven't seen her."

True. A chill raced over me. "The witches outside told me she came in here. The hunters let her in."

Her expression was impassive. "That may be true. I've been inside this room for most of the afternoon, except during the time I went to check in with the guards at the gates. As for Rebecca's sister, I imagine she came to plead her sister's case."

"She... I don't think she's here. Someone wanted her out of the way. Not all the hunters here are on your side."

"That's what you believe?" She shook her head. "I suppose I cannot blame you for being paranoid, given the system you exist in. The process for governing the covens is rife with potential for corruption, and I have to admit I'm surprised something like this didn't happen sooner. Murder of two Head Witches... by a child, no less."

"Did you not hear a word I said about it being physically impossible for Rebecca to have murdered Brenna?" The words snapped out before I could stop them. "Let alone Coral, since Rebecca didn't have any knowledge of the curse used to kill either of them. And she wouldn't use her magic for anything like that. She never wanted to use that power to hurt anyone. That was all her mother."

She cocked a brow. "I hope you don't expect me to take your word for it on that, Blair. I've heard much the same from your coven leader, but you're prone to the same biases, and none of you can be trusted."

"Speak for yourself," I said. "There're a dozen Head Witches here with more motive to have committed both crimes if you'd look away from *your* biases for five minutes. And if you want to root out corruption, then I'd suggest you look to your own people first."

"Your own history does you no favours, Blair Wilkes," said Linda. "Especially your tendency to intervene in hunters' business."

"You mean when I exposed your leader as a fairy who'd been duping you all for years?" I couldn't believe what I was hearing. "How is that less corrupt than the system for picking Head Witches? At least a sceptre picking the person who wields it can't have human biases the way the people who voted *him* into power did."

Linda's face flushed with anger or perhaps embarrassment. She might be in complete denial about Rebecca's innocence, but she couldn't deny that the hunters had made a major mistake in trusting their leader throughout the past few years and that they were far from incorruptible.

Before either of us could speak another word, the door flew open. Two hunters entered, one of whom had been guarding the front doors, while a commotion sounded from the background. I recognised Robin shouting, accompanied by outraged squeaking noises. *Tansy. Oh no.*

"We've heard a disturbing report about you, Blair," said one of the hunters. "It sounds like you've been attempting to contact one of our high-security prisoners."

I froze. "Excuse me? Who said that?"

"Was that an admission?"

"Of course not," I said. "Do I look like I have the means of contacting anyone? We're not allowed to leave, are we?"

A third hunter entered the room—whose trouser leg was torn to shreds as if by an angry squirrel—and held up the note I'd left in the flower bed. "This is an attempt to contact the mother of the accused."

My heart lurched. Judging by the state of his uniform, I knew he'd picked up the note himself and Tansy had tailed him here. Did that mean *he* was the one who'd intended to take the note to Mrs Dailey, or had someone ratted me out to the hunters and caused the ones who didn't support her to unearth my reply? Not Robin, surely, but the other witches were hardly my biggest fans. *I should never have replied in the first place.*

"Interesting," said Linda Graham. "Thank you for that, Barker. What exactly happened to your clothes?"

"Her friend's familiar attacked me." The hunter—Barker —pointed accusingly at me.

"I have no intention of working with Mrs Dailey." I glared straight back at him. "She was trying to blackmail *Rebecca* into working with her, and after Rebecca refused to reply, someone locked her familiar in a spare room to keep him from giving away who her messenger was. Robin and I came up with a plan to expose them by leaving a fake reply to her latest message."

More hunters had gathered outside the questioning room, and my heart gave a lurch when I spotted Nathan among them. His eyes were wide, horrified, but he didn't speak a word. Was he not going to stand up for me even now?

"What exactly is going on here?" Madame Grey's voice drifted from behind the hunters, who pulled back as she came marching into view, wearing her most severe expression.

Of all the timing. I still needed to talk to her but not in front of the crowd of hunters—not to mention the witches from outside, several of whom had ascended the steps outside the front door to hear what was going on.

"One of your witches has been found to be communicating with a high-security prisoner," Barker told Madame Grey.

"The prisoner in question was trying to blackmail Rebecca," I said quickly. "I found a note from her in the flower bed, and since Rebecca isn't capable of replying even if she wanted to, I took it upon myself to find out who's delivering notes on behalf of the prisoner by writing a reply."

"A likely story," said Linda in an apparent attempt to regain control of the situation. "You left a reply to the prisoner accepting her offer of an alliance, didn't you?"

"You can read the note yourself as proof that's not true," I said. "It doesn't say anything about collaborating with her.

I wanted to find the identity of her delivery boy... and it looks like I found him." I pointed at Barker.

"Nonsense!" he exclaimed. "She wants to help her friend wriggle out of facing justice, so she's making up lies."

"You know justice has nothing to do with your decision to blame Rebecca." To Linda, I added, "Now do you see what I meant about someone in your own ranks working against you? Who do you think put that note from Mrs Dailey in the flower bed to begin with?"

"I don't see any note from her," she said, unblinking. "The only note I see is yours."

I should have seen that one coming. "Her note was enchanted to fall apart as soon as it was read, but you know perfectly well that I'm the one who put her in that cell to begin with. I have no interest in accepting her help, and neither do her daughters. I only found the note in the first place because I was looking for Blythe—who seems to have disappeared. Has anyone seen her?"

Madame Grey's attention sharpened at that. "Disappeared?"

"More lies," said Linda.

"According to one of the witches, she went off with one of the hunters, along with Rebecca's familiar." I drew in a breath. "I think the hunter in question is allied with Mrs Dailey and took her to force Rebecca's hand—and mine."

"That is a serious accusation," said Linda. "Which hunter, exactly?"

"I didn't see them." I looked desperately at Madame Grey, willing her to believe me. "Toast—Rebecca's familiar—was the recipient of the first note Mrs Dailey gave to her daughter. Soon after that, he disappeared, and I found him locked in an upstairs room. I think someone realised that Robin's ability to communicate with animals might be able to expose who gave him the note. Then the second one turned up in the flower bed—"

"This is a waste of time," said the hunter whose leg had been clawed up.

"I agree," said Linda. "I'm intrigued to know what you think of Blair's behaviour, however, Madame Grey. Is it typical of your coven?"

My face heated, but Madame Grey appeared unbothered by her mocking tone.

"I have no knowledge of anything Blair has been doing while I was in the council room," she said in calm tones. "I told you already that I believe Rebecca to be innocent, but her mother certainly shouldn't be able to communicate with anyone. If it's true, that's another matter entirely and out of the scope of my power to investigate."

Is that all? She couldn't have given up, but maybe she'd had to put her focus on proving Rebecca's innocence without any space for anything else. The hunters had trapped her too.

"I see," said Linda. "I've questioned Blair myself, and she believes herself to be acting righteously, but the answers are clear. I believe it's time to declare that the formal investigation is over."

"What does that mean?" I asked, alarmed. "You aren't arresting Rebecca."

"She'll have a fair trial," said Linda. "Especially since she's a minor. Don't worry yourself."

"That's ridiculous," I said. "Are you going to completely overlook the fact that one of your hunters is delivering messages on behalf of a high-security prisoner?"

"You have no proof of any of our people being involved," Linda said.

"Ask your hunter why he was digging around in the flower beds." I pointed at Barker in desperation.

"One of your fellow witches mentioned your suspicious behaviour," Barker said. "Then another witch's familiar attacked me when I found your note. If you ask me, I ought to press charges for assault."

Oh no. Had I got Robin and her familiar into trouble as well? She'd done her best to help me, but she was almost as out of her depth here as I was, despite being a Head Witch. I could only imagine what her mother would say if she and Tansy got into trouble for assaulting a hunter, even one who'd deserved it, but ultimately, it was Rebecca whom the hunters had been set against from the start.

"If you like," said Linda. "I imagine the other witches will be pleased when I tell them they can finally leave the property and return to their homes."

"You're letting a killer walk free." My hands curled into fists, anger sparking in my veins. "You're exploiting every loophole in the magical laws for your own gain. You can't expect to get away with this."

"If we are, it doesn't say much for the laws, does it?" Linda gave me a pitying look. "As for you, Blair, I think you should go and spend some time alone and calm down before you implicate yourself even further."

Two hunters closed in on either side of me, driving me backwards into the questioning room. I lunged forwards, but one of them seized my wand from my hand before retreating from the room. The instant the door closed, I heard a key turn in the lock, sealing me inside.

This was it. I was trapped, Rebecca was doomed to be arrested, and even Madame Grey couldn't do a thing to help either of us. The hunters had won, and Mrs Dailey had too.

I sank into the empty seat, putting my head in my hands,

and listened to the sound of Linda and the others walking away, presumably to break the good news to the other witches—except for Rebecca.

Raised voices made my head snap upward. It took a moment before I recognised one of the voices as Nathan's.

"This won't stand," he said in a sharp voice. "You want to pin the blame entirely on Blair and not investigate who among our own ranks left the note? There's either a collaborator with a high-security prisoner in one of our jails or someone pretending to be such, and I won't stand by while they undermine everything that we've fought for in the last decades of bringing criminals to justice."

My heart began to beat faster. Finally, he was arguing for me... though far too late to be of any use.

"A nice sentiment, but you've been apart from the hunters for years, Nathan," a hunter replied. "Your family is biased."

"I know what the hunters used to stand for," he said. "Whoever is passing on messages from prisoners attempting to blackmail people—if that is indeed what they're doing—certainly doesn't represent the hunters. I'd like to know who's involved, wouldn't you?"

"We have more pressing issues, Nathan," the hunter said. "Once we have the culprit transferred to jail, we'll see to your girlfriend. If she manages to keep her mouth shut this time, she'll get to walk free. That clear?"

His reply was cold. "Crystal. You'd better keep your word."

I heard his footsteps receding and sat back down, tears pricking my eyes. He'd left me in here, but the hunters had given him no choice. If he'd kept arguing, he might have found himself locked up alongside me. Madame Grey was in a bind too. It'd take all her clout to get Rebecca out of a lifelong sentence, but who else was left to find the truth?

"Sky," I whispered. "I guess you're not going to show up, then. I hope you're having fun, wherever you are."

I didn't know why I was talking to him from inside a locked room when he wasn't even on the property. It was absurd.

A faint noise came from nearby. I lifted my head and glimpsed a dark blur in the corner of my eye.

Sky sat there, against the back wall, looking for all the world as if he'd been in there the whole time.

14

———

"Sky." Casually wandering into a locked room was just like my familiar, but where on earth had he been all this time?

I startled when a crash echoed from somewhere else in the house, like a door slamming, and several thuds followed. They sounded close enough to the room that I backed up a step, wishing I had my wand—and the door flew open.

Erin, Nathan's sister, stood in the entryway, and next to her lay the bodies of two unconscious hunters.

"Sorry I got here so late," she said. "I was out hiking."

I stared at her then at Sky, who rubbed against my legs, purring. "You... you what?"

"Your cat was very persistent in looking for Buck and me." Erin held out my wand, and I took it on autopilot, dazed. "He followed us around, yowling until I called Nathan and found out what was going on here."

"Nathan has been in contact, has he?" My tone sounded sharper than I'd intended, given that my boyfriend's bizarre behaviour was the least of my current preoccupations.

"Yeah, he has." She raised a brow, apparently surprised

at my tone. "When he wasn't busy fobbing off the hunters in the hopes of catching the traitor in the act. I think he's dealing with that now."

"Dealing with what?" Okay, I was way behind. "What *are* you doing here? Where are the rest of the hunters?"

A grin flitted across her mouth. "Madame Grey set up a diversion that'll keep them occupied for a while. Want to come out before these two guys wake up?"

I walked out of the room, too bewildered to do anything but stare around the entrance hall. "Is Rebecca still locked up?"

Her smile faded. "That's where the hunters went. They took her into custody at their local base, and Madame Grey followed to ensure they don't come back. Don't worry. She and Buck are keeping an eye on them."

"What?" My voice rose, and she shushed me.

"I don't know whether any of them are still roaming around the house, so keep it down," she said. "Relax. They won't do anything to Rebecca while Buck's watching them. I won't let them—and neither will Nathan."

"Give me one reason to trust either of you at the moment."

"Ouch," she said. "My brother did too good a job at keeping his distance, did he? You can talk to him later, but *I'm* here, and pretty much everyone in Fairy Falls knows someone from the hunters has gone rogue. As soon as we heard Rebecca was framed *and* blackmailed, it didn't take a genius to connect the dots and assume foul play."

"But—look, you know this originally started with two murders, don't you?" It didn't matter what the others in Fairy Falls thought as long as they weren't here to help. "The killer's getting away scot-free while the hunters pin the blame on Rebecca and claim this mess as proof the Head

Witches' system doesn't work and that they should take the covens' place."

"I know. Don't worry." She looked behind her. "Oh, here's that foolish brother of mine."

Nathan strode straight past her and pulled me into a hug. I found myself hugging him back by sheer instinct and forced myself to pull away. "What are you playing at?"

He reached for my hand, his mouth turning down at the corners. "Blair. I'm sorry I didn't intervene sooner. I didn't expect them to lock you up."

"But you expected the rest?" The words burst out despite the urgency of the situation. "You let them arrest Rebecca and treat us both like dirt. In fact, you did some of that yourself."

"Like I said, too good at acting," Erin cut in. "If you ask me, you should have gone into the theatre instead of joining the security team."

Nathan ignored his sister and hugged me again, drawing a muffled objection that turned into a sob. "That's not fair. You can't hug me while I'm emotionally compromised."

"Never again," he murmured. "This was the hardest thing I've ever had to do."

I blinked back tears. "Was it worth it?"

He drew in a breath. "If you and Rebecca are able to escape without punishment, it's worth it to both of us, isn't it?"

"There's no proof that'll happen." My voice cracked. "It's too late."

"It isn't," Nathan insisted. "I caught the hunter who's been communicating with Mrs Dailey from behind the scenes, and he's currently locked in a broom cupboard. Does that help?"

"You know... yes, it does." This time, I returned the hug, too relieved to stay angry with him.

"Come *on*," Erin said from by my shoulder. "Catch up later. We have a prisoner to interrogate."

"Yeah. We do." The relief of having Nathan back on my side momentarily eclipsed my worries, not to mention my confusion at the absence of anyone in the lobby aside from the two unconscious hunters who'd been guarding my room.

"Where is everyone?" I asked Nathan. "Won't the hunters come back after they realise Madame Grey distracted them?"

"That's why we need to move fast. He's this way."

I followed him and Erin while Sky padded behind me as if he hadn't scared me half to death by showing up out of nowhere. Like Nathan, he'd had my back from the start. I needed to do better to remember that.

One of the unconscious guards stirred a little, and Erin moved towards him. "I'll keep an eye on these guys."

"How did you plan on not being arrested for assault?" I asked her.

"They don't know me," said Erin. "We'll be long gone by the time they think to check up on us, and I think they have bigger problems on their hands."

Nathan pushed open a nearby door, revealing a narrow cupboard in which Barker sat on the floor, his trousers still torn to shreds from Tansy's claws. *I knew it was him.*

He lifted his head. "I expected this kind of behaviour from you, Blair Wilkes, but I'm disappointed that you've even lured several former hunters into believing your lies."

"My what?" I asked blankly. "You're the one who's been passing on messages from Mrs Dailey while pretending to be loyal to the hunters, aren't you? You can't accuse *me* of lying with a straight face."

"I beg to differ," he said. "Sometimes, lies are necessary for the greater good."

"I'm not following." I glanced at Nathan, who looked equally perplexed. "What do you have to gain from working with Mrs Dailey in the first place? Why blackmail Rebecca on her behalf?"

"Like I said." He pushed himself into a sitting position. "It's an effective way to show where her loyalties truly lie."

"Rebecca's?" I frowned. "You're not serious, are you? Even if you ignore the blackmail part, you broke the law in delivering notes from a high-security prisoner to the outside world."

"Sometimes, bending the laws is necessary for the purposes of exposing treachery. You've done some of that yourself, Blair, haven't you?"

My lie-sensing power detected no untruths. He wasn't lying, but he was deluding himself at the very least. Had Mrs Dailey even written the notes at all? Or had he forged them with his own hand?

"You think the hunters will care for the technicalities?" I shook my head at him. "You didn't just break the laws. You helped the real killer get away with their crimes. The least you can do is tell me who really killed Coral and Brenna."

"Your friend did. Or she might as well have."

"You know perfectly well that isn't true." My voice dropped. "She was set up. Did you make a deal with another Head Witch to cover for them by framing Rebecca?"

"Certainly not." He sounded affronted. "Your friend didn't need to be framed to appear guilty."

"Then you don't know who the killer is?" If not, then he was simply an opportunist who'd taken advantage of Rebecca's predicament to pull this bizarre loyalty test on her. For all I knew, he'd never spoken to Mrs Dailey at all. It was all for show.

"It hardly matters who the killer is. I thought you would have realised by now."

"This is a power grab," Nathan said from behind me. "Granted, you aren't the only one who tried to take advantage of the situation, but you went too far. Even Linda will see that."

"She's far too busy to care," he said dismissively.

"Does *she* know who the killer is?" I asked.

"I haven't the faintest idea."

"You're something else, you are." If this guy was solely responsible for the blackmail, then he must be responsible for Blythe's and Toast's ill-timed disappearances too. "What did you do with Blythe, then?"

"Who?"

"Rebecca's sister. And her familiar too. You're the one who lured them away from that flower bed so you could leave the note, right?"

"No." He lifted his chin in defiance. "They were already gone when I slipped the note in."

True.

"Then who?" I tensed when a groan came from one of the unconscious guards behind me. We were almost out of time. "A hunter took them. If not you, then who?"

"Who told you that?" asked Nathan.

I thought back. "Meredith said they came into the house..."

"Time's up," Erin said impatiently. "Leave him in there. We have to get out of here before those guys wake up."

"And go where?" I stepped back as Nathan shut the door on Barker. "We still haven't found the killer... or the truth."

"The other witches are outside." Nathan turned the key in the lock, sealing the hunter in his room. "I forgot to mention Madame Grey stepped in and cast a spell to lock both the front and back gates after Linda and the others left with Rebecca."

"Good. The killer is still somewhere on the property." My heart gave a lurch. "Wait, are the Head Witches' sceptres still locked up somewhere in here?"

A crash resounded through the lobby, the front doors bouncing off their frames as Arabella Knotgrass herself came striding in, her mouth taut with rage. "What are you doing in my house? I should have you all arrested."

"Meaning me?" Erin asked. "I'm a former hunter and a member of Fairy Falls's security team, which means I'm included in your invitation to the hunters."

"That's correct," Nathan stepped in. "It's my understanding that the leader of the Knotgrass Coven gave her express permission for the hunters to enter the house and take over the investigation. If I'm included in that invitation, then so is Erin."

"I thought you didn't want the hunters here," I said to Arabella. "I thought you wanted them gone."

I'd also thought they'd invited themselves when Nathan had called the police, not that Arabella herself had given them permission to invade her property and take over the questioning.

"The agreement was that they were to leave as soon as they found the culprit," Arabella said haughtily. "Which means the two of you are still trespassing."

"So are they." Erin gestured to the unconscious hunters. "When they wake up, I'm sure they'll tell me all about how you handed the keys over to Linda yourself. There's no point in denying it."

Anger flared in Arabella's eyes. "Fine. I believe the Head Witches are a corrupt organisation and that one of them murdering another on my property was reason enough to let another authority step in. Would you not have done the same?"

"Did *you* kill Coral and Brenna?" I couldn't help asking.

"No, of course not," she snapped. "But as this past day has proven, no Head Witch is deserving of their title nor of the power they wield. I didn't want these to be the circumstances in which I proved that to be true, but it is what it is."

"I suppose the hunters offered your coven special treatment if you supported Linda Graham's rise to power," I said. "The same as Mrs Dailey."

"Don't you dare compare me to *her*." She reached for her wand—and froze, her mouth partly open and her hand in her pocket.

"Sorry to interrupt." Robin stepped around her. "I thought she was likely to keep talking for a while."

"What did you do to her?" asked Erin.

"I used a freeze-frame spell." Robin held up her sceptre. "I'm still learning moderation, but it comes in handy in situations like this. She'll be stuck like that for hours if I don't undo it."

"Nice going," I said. "Hours, though? It's not going to take that long to find the killer."

"You still don't know who it is?" She looked at the unconscious hunters. "You found the person blackmailing you, at least?"

"Yes, but he isn't working with the killer," I explained quickly. "Also, Blythe and Toast are still missing, and he doesn't know where they are."

Robin's expression shadowed. "Nobody can leave the house or the grounds. All the other witches are outside.

Want me to find a way to torment them until someone snaps and confesses?"

"If they didn't crack under the hunters' interrogations, there's no guarantees," I said. "Where's Tansy?"

"Watching the gates to warn me if the other hunters come back. Madame Grey led them on a wild chase after she locked everyone else in here."

"So that's where she is." Unfortunately, that meant she wasn't *here*, and we still hadn't found the actual killer. "I need to find Meredith. She's the one who told me Blythe and Toast came back into the house... though now I think about it, she didn't mention they went with the hunters."

I sidestepped the frozen Arabella and walked out the door, surveying the witches gathered in the garden below. They'd broken into groups, some huddled together, others arguing about the indignity of being locked up. The nearest witch, Catherine Oakley, peered up at me. "Where has that coven leader of yours gone to? I'll have her reported for locking us up, I will."

I brushed off her comment. "Where's Meredith?"

"Her?" asked Catherine Oakley. "She went back into the house before Arabella did. Now, listen to me—"

"She did?" I left her midrant and hurried back through the open doors to the house.

There, Robin waylaid me. "We have a problem."

"What problem?"

"Someone else has been in there and taken one of the sceptres." She indicated an open door to a small storeroom, in which I glimpsed the other Head Witches' sceptres lined up on the desk. "I don't know when they got in, but I didn't realise until I counted them."

My heart dropped like a stone. "I think I know whose is missing."

15

"We need to find her," I told Erin, Nathan, and Robin. "Meredith's the only person unaccounted for, and if she's taken her sceptre back too..."

How can she be the killer? How can it be her?

"She can't have left the house," Robin said. "I didn't see her when I came in. Did any of you?"

"No," said Nathan. "I was with the hunters until Erin showed up."

"And ambushed those two." Erin indicated the two unconscious hunters. "We can ask our prisoner, but I doubt *he* was paying attention. How about her?"

I followed her gaze to Arabella, who remained frozen to the spot. "Robin, you can set her free, can't you?"

Robin gave me a dubious look. "Yes, but she's not going to improve the situation."

"She knows how the house's magic operates," I reminded her. "And I reckon our killer does too. We already know it isn't Arabella, whatever agenda she had when she invited the hunters here."

"Fair enough." Robin pointed the sceptre at her. "I'll free her, but I vote we disarm her first."

"Easy enough." Erin snatched Arabella's wand from her frozen hand. "I'll hang on to this until I'm sure she isn't going to put a curse on Blair."

"Might be too much to hope for." Despite her frozen state, I could swear Arabella's eyes were fixed directly on me. "If she doesn't cooperate with us, who else knows their way around the house? We don't have much time."

"You mean to find our missing persons?" Robin backed towards the door. "I'll send Tansy to scout around and see if she can pick up Blythe's scent. Or Meredith's. Whichever works."

"Miaow." Sky stepped into view, as if to say, *Hey, I can hunt for her, if you haven't forgotten I'm here.* Which I had, admittedly, because he'd been inconveniently absent until he'd shown up out of nowhere.

"I think Sky is volunteering too."

Robin eyed my cat with interest. "That's your familiar?"

"Miaow," said Sky.

"Yeah," I said. "You can understand him, right?"

"You know... no, I can't. Weird. What kind of cat is he?"

Wait. Her ability doesn't work on him? "I thought you could understand all animals."

"Almost all. He's not a shifter, is he?"

"No, he's a fairy cat."

Her brows shot up. "A fairy cat? I've never met one of those before."

"Miaow," said Sky.

"I think that means 'Yes, I'm unique,'" I said to her. "He has his own way of communicating with me, and he should be able to find Blythe and Meredith."

"Miaow." Sky approached the stairs and hopped onto

the banister as if he intended to pursue the killer himself. His ability to walk through walls and make himself unseen meant he'd be able to get anywhere in the house, and it didn't hurt that if he ran into trouble, he'd be able to glamour himself to look like a giant monster.

I didn't share those advantages, but I couldn't help feeling partly responsible for Blythe's predicament. She'd distrusted Meredith from the get-go, while I'd never thought her hatred of Mrs Dailey would lead to her trying to frame one of her daughters for murder.

What if she'd done worse to the other? I didn't like Blythe, but I didn't want her to die.

Behind me, Robin cleared her throat. "I'm just going to bring Tansy in here, then I'll undo the spell on our delightful host and see what she knows."

"Thanks." I heard a thumping noise and looked sharply behind me, but it was just Erin closing a classroom door.

"I locked our two hunter friends in there," she explained. "That way, they won't cause trouble while we're searching the house. Nathan, want to help?"

Nathan eyed me. "I'll go with Blair, wherever she wants to go."

A flush heated my face when everyone turned towards me. "You should help your sister. We don't want those hunters getting out."

I wished we could have a private moment to talk, but there was no time, and before I knew it, Robin was back, with Tansy scurrying at her feet.

"Ready?" She pointed the sceptre at Arabella. "We have approximately two minutes to question her before my mother comes in and finds out I've used my sceptre against another witch. I'd really prefer not to have to freeze *her* too."

"We'll see if we can avoid it." I nodded. "Set her free."

A flick of the sceptre, and Arabella staggered forward, her eyes widening. "How dare you attack me!"

"You tried to attack Blair," Erin called from across the hall, twirling Arabella's confiscated wand between her fingers.

"That's mine!" Arabella said. "Give that back."

"I have a question," I said. "After I've asked it, you're welcome to take your wand and leave. Also, I believe there's a killer on the loose in your house."

"What?" She goggled at me. "Are you mocking me?"

"No, and here's my question," I said. "Does Meredith Norwood know her way around your house?"

"Meredith?" she echoed. "Why her?"

"She's the one witch who's currently unaccounted for. She was spotted coming back into the house, and her sceptre's missing. She hated Mrs Dailey, perhaps badly enough to take it out on her daughters. I don't know why she killed Coral and Brenna, but that's not what I asked."

She shook her head slowly. "You can't be serious. *She* isn't the killer."

"Does she know the way around your house?" I repeated. "Despite the redecoration spell?"

The colour drained from her face. "She asked for a private tour before the meeting."

My throat went dry. "Good to know. I'm pretty sure she's taken Blythe hostage and Rebecca's familiar too. Where's she likely to have stashed them?"

"What...?" She jumped when one of the hunters slammed against the classroom door from the inside. "Where are the hunters? Did you lock them up?"

"Temporarily," said Robin. "Their only agenda is to further their ambitions, not investigate the murders. With your help, it seems."

A flush smothered Arabella's face. "I did no such thing."

"You all but admitted you did," I said. "More importantly, you might have a dangerous killer loose in your own coven's headquarters. I'll ask again... where might she be hiding?"

Her face paled again. "That's not... she wouldn't have."

"Miaow." Sky was back, as if he'd never left, and he used his tail to beckon me towards the stairs.

"He found her." I made to follow him. "Who's coming with me?"

"Wait just one second," Arabella objected.

But I left Robin to deal with her. Their argument faded into the background as I followed Sky upstairs. Erin and Nathan would have their hands full keeping the hunters from escaping their rooms, let alone figuring out how to avoid our getting blamed for attacking them.

That left it to me to find Meredith. With Sky at my side, I made my way to the upper floor, where I'd found Toast locked inside one of the many offices. As before, four corridors stretched out diagonally, lined with closed doors.

"Which way?" I whispered to Sky.

In answer, he led me down the left-hand corridor on silent paw steps until he came to a lone wooden door at the very end of the corridor. I assumed it must be locked like the others, but on the other side, I heard a murmuring voice. *Meredith's?*

I pulled out my wand with one hand and reached for the door with the other—then hesitated. Was I making a mistake in coming here alone? I'd never fought someone who held a sceptre before, but they were far more powerful than a regular wand, and I'd barely passed my Grade Four magical exams.

I was no match for a fully trained Head Witch, and there

was a good chance I'd be dead the instant I stepped through that door.

Sky nudged my foot, a reminder that I wasn't alone. I doubted she'd be expecting a fairy cat, at the very least... or a fairy witch either.

As a witch, I didn't stand a chance against Meredith, but I wasn't just a witch.

"Go in," I whispered to Sky. "Sneak up on her. Disarm her if you can."

If he got that sceptre away from her, we'd be on a more even footing. Sky slipped through the door while I snapped my fingers and brought out my fairy wings. The sudden absence of my glamour brought a sense of vulnerability, but I threw a new glamour over myself with another snap of my fingers, rendering myself invisible.

Following Sky's lead, I pushed the door open and stepped through into a long room that contained a single cabinet and nothing else. My gaze picked out Meredith in the darkness. She was standing with her back to me without noticing Sky's unseen approach.

Then I spotted Blythe sitting against the far wall, her wrists and ankles restrained with ropes, with poor Toast trembling at her feet.

"Miaow," Sky called out.

Toast meowed back miserably. My heart dropped when Meredith stiffened, turning around, but her gaze skimmed over my invisible form and fixated on Sky. He'd appeared at her feet, looking for all the world like a harmless familiar.

"Who are you?" Meredith asked Sky. "I haven't seen you before. Someone's familiar, are you?"

"Great deduction there," Blythe scoffed. "I wondered if you forgot you're in another coven's house."

Meredith pursed her lips. "Maybe I should have gagged

you. You have nothing useful to share with me, do you? I really thought your mother would have told you *something*, but I suppose it was your sister who was more useful to her."

What's she talking about? Did she want some information only Mrs Dailey had? If so, why not ask Rebecca instead of capturing her sister? None of this made sense, and neither did the nearly empty room she'd chosen to hide herself in. The only piece of furniture was that single towering cabinet. I assumed it must be valuable... or its contents were.

"What do you even plan on doing with me?" Blythe asked. "You can't expect the others not to notice I'm gone."

"You have your own coven leader to thank for distracting them," said Meredith. "Besides, I doubt any of them will have missed you, even your sister. She has bigger problems on her hands."

Blythe struggled upright and cursed. "She's been arrested for crimes *you* committed. You're sick. You know that?"

That much, I agreed with. Ignoring her, Meredith crouched in front of Sky. "If you're reporting to that Robin, I'm afraid I'll have to restrain you as well. We can't have you telling tales."

"I bet that stumped you." Blythe's tone turned mocking. "You didn't realise the animals would tell tales on you, did you?"

"I knew of the Wildwood Coven's abilities before I came here." Meredith spoke in calm tones. "I know the powers of all the Head Witches, including your sister. That's why it was so very easy to set this up."

But why? It might be too much to hope that Meredith would reveal her motives before she tried to restrain Sky and found out the hard way why that was a terrible idea, but when Blythe briefly looked in my direction, I figured that she'd known as soon as she'd seen Sky that he wasn't alone in here. *Please don't give me away, Blythe.*

"Yes, you're a genius, clearly." Blythe rolled her eyes at Meredith. "You killed two people for no good reason. Because you hate your job. It must be so taxing, being one of the most powerful witches in the country."

"I don't dislike the power and prestige that comes with the title." She studied the sceptre in her hand for a moment. "I *do* think there's a major problem with putting almost the entirety of the magical world's power in the hands of a few inept individuals. If two of those inept individuals had to die to prove my point, that's just too bad."

"Wow." Blythe struggled against her bonds. Was she trying to tease out Meredith's motives too? Maybe she was trying to keep Meredith's attention on her because she assumed I had a plan.

I'd thought *Sky* had a plan. I caught his eye, knowing that he at least could see my hiding place, and mouthed, "Scare her."

At my command, Sky turned into his monstrous form and leapt onto Meredith from behind. She stumbled forward, the sceptre dropping from her hand. Seizing my chance, I cast a spell that undid Blythe's bonds, but Meredith dodged Sky's paws and lunged for the sceptre again.

Sky got there first, leaping over her head. His paws pinned the long instrument to the ground. Meredith and I both dove at it at the same time.

Meredith reached into her pocket. A flare of light shot from her wand, and I found myself flying backwards, my body slamming into the wall.

"I should have known it was you." She flicked her wand at Sky, who tumbled over and landed at my feet.

"Sky!" I shouted, alarmed, as Meredith picked up the sceptre.

The glow ignited in her hands while I struggled to catch my breath. I would've thought her sceptre would be less quick to answer her command after she'd used it to commit multiple murders, but if the hunters had got one thing right, it was acknowledging that depending on a sceptre wasn't the best way to determine who was worthy to be Head Witch.

Then again, regular people weren't infallible either. One just needed to look at Arabella and the way she'd let the hunters into her home, Linda Graham's abuse of her leadership position, and everything Mrs Dailey had done, whether she'd ever been involved in this situation or not.

When Meredith pointed the sceptre at me, Blythe tackled her from behind. The sceptre fell from her hands for a second time, and Toast leapt in, sending the pointed instrument skidding underneath the cabinet.

"No!" She ran towards the cabinet, but Sky barred her path, his huge, monstrous form blocking her way forward. A rumbling growl escaped from him.

"Hey!" Robin came running into the room behind me, and in a wave of her sceptre, Meredith froze on the spot.

Sky growled again then turned back into his ordinary-sized self. "Miaow."

Toast meowed, too, while Robin raised a brow at me. "You're full of surprises. You know that?"

"You don't know the half of it." I directed part of that to Meredith, who remained frozen with her back to the door, her hands inches from the cabinet. "Her sceptre's underneath there. I don't know what's in that cabinet, but I think she was trying to steal it."

Arabella entered the room. "She wouldn't have succeeded," she answered in a tremulous voice. "It's not possible."

Behind her, Nathan and Erin walked in, surveying Meredith's frozen form.

"Got her," Erin said. "Nice job, Blair."

"Robin's the one who froze her." I turned to Arabella. "What *is* in that cabinet, anyway?"

She spoke after a long pause. "A portal to Fairyland."

16

After the bombshell she'd dropped, I had even more questions about Arabella's house than I did concerning the murder, but when Madame Grey came striding upstairs, she ordered the rest of us to vacate the room. I snapped my fingers and switched from fairy mode back to witch mode, then we supervised Meredith's being moved to a downstairs room and then went to bring the hunters in to witness her confession—including the ones Erin had knocked out.

Robin had offered to alter their memories of the events so that they'd think Meredith had knocked them out instead, but I figured we had more important matters to deal with than one of their former members getting a little over-enthusiastic with setting me free. Nathan and Erin said they didn't mind taking the heat, though it was safe to say Nathan's attempt to get in with the hunters again had officially crashed and burned.

I wouldn't lie. I was glad of it.

In any case, the hunters had their hands full, listening to Arabella's revelation that Meredith had been the killer all along. Her confession had had too many witnesses to deny, even for Linda Graham, who showed up shortly after Nathan had freed the two hunters from their brief imprisonment, breathless and fuming.

"I turn my back for five minutes, and you all completely lose your ability to do your jobs?" she asked the two bewildered hunters. "Where are the others?" She addressed the question to Madame Grey. "What did you do?"

"I simply ensured my fellow witches had a clear path to find your murderer," said Madame Grey. "When you arrested the wrong person, I knew the real killer would believe they'd got away with their crimes, so I took it upon myself to take over your defences around the property. Even then, the killer managed to steal back the sceptre from under the noses of your fellow hunters."

The two hunters spluttered in protest, but they quietened under Linda's withering stare.

"You knew the killer's identity all along, and you never told me?" she asked of Madame Grey.

"No, I did not," Madame Grey said. "I *did* know the killer was likely to strike again, given the chance, and after you locked Blair up and prevented her from following my orders to help find the killer, it was even more important that I did everything I could to keep everyone safe."

"If this Meredith Norwood is the killer, then what reasoning did she give for her crimes?" Linda asked.

"Has everyone forgotten she tried to steal from my house?" Arabella exploded. "I brought your hunters in here with the understanding that you'd do the bare minimum to keep order. Instead, you let the murderer walk away and almost unleashed disaster."

In what way? If Meredith had been intending to steal the cabinet, she must have had a way to get it out of here, unless this so-called portal to Fairyland was much smaller than the actual cabinet was. But my list of questions about the cabinet would have to wait. Once everyone had filled Linda in on the events she'd missed, she was left to question Meredith herself while we all waited for the rest of the hunters to return—with Rebecca.

Blythe ran off to give them a reminder to get a move on, while the rest of us ended up back in the garden once we'd given an account of our conflict with Meredith. Now Madame Grey had taken charge of the situation, Linda had to cede control. *Pity for her.*

"This isn't over," I murmured to Robin. "We have three Head Witches who need replacing. That's going to cause some ripples."

"Exactly," said Robin. "The hunters have a lot to answer for as well."

Some of the other witches had already started to debate about who'd take Meredith's place—not to mention Coral's and Brenna's—and their bickering was starting to give me a headache. To be honest, I wasn't sure if any of the people present were qualified to carry their *own* sceptres—even the non-Head Witches, like Arabella Knotgrass, who'd invited the hunters into her house while feigning ignorance.

"Arabella isn't the only one who'd be willing to make a deal with the hunters to keep her coven safe," I said. "She's more like Mrs Dailey than she's willing to admit."

"I feel bad for Rebecca," said Robin. "I have some scheming relatives of my own, but at least my mother isn't one of them. Though my mum's going to be furious that I used the sceptre to freeze a fellow coven leader."

"She needs to get her priorities in order, then," I said. "You saved my neck in there."

Tansy squeaked from her shoulder, and Robin gave a

faint laugh. "Tansy says I'm the best of the Head Witches... which is worrying more than anything else. I won't lie."

"At least Meredith is going to lose her title," I said. "Glad to know committing murder is enough of a good reason to be stripped of one's sceptre. I was kind of worried it wouldn't be."

"I know, right?" she said. "The more I learn about this Head Witch thing, the more I question whoever set the system up to begin with."

"I guess they assumed everyone would obey the laws to the letter and be willing to act for the good of the covens." I rolled my eyes.

"Not really. The original rules were more based around consolidating power, from what I've read," Robin said. "The sceptres used to stay within certain families, but that was unfair for obvious reasons, so the councils voted to expand the number of people who can put themselves forward as potential candidates for Head Witch. That doesn't mean the original covens were happy about it, though. In fact, every change they've made has been met with complaints, including when they moved the Head Witch ceremony to Samhain."

I blinked in surprise. "You mean it used to be on a different date?"

"Sure," she said. "A sceptre can pick a new Head Witch at any moment, technically, but a few hundred years ago, the covens came to an agreement to nominate one day per year on which to hold the ceremony. This kind of situation— when a Head Witch retires early, dies, or is convicted of murder—is an exception."

I frowned. "Doesn't that mean any Head Witch is allowed to resign their position if they wanted to?"

I didn't know if Rebecca had considered that option.

There hadn't exactly been a lot of other candidates available—and I had to admit I wasn't overly keen on the idea of her being replaced by Stephanie Underhill—but being Head Witch had been more trouble than it was worth, and she was far too young for this level of responsibility.

"It's not that common for them to do so without good reason," she said. "And it's such a fraught issue with the covens that nobody really talks about it. I only know because I've been researching loopholes since I got roped into the job."

"You want to quit?" I kept my voice low, surprised to hear her admit it—or not, given that like Rebecca, she'd had the worst possible impression of the other Head Witches at her first meeting. People like Meredith, who abused the rules to cling to their power, seemed to be the norm, not the exception.

"No, but I like to have options." Robin lowered her voice too. "Anyway, the covens like their traditions. I can guarantee they'll want to keep all this quiet, so there'll be a new Head Witch in Meredith's place by the end of the week, and that'll be that."

"I'd be surprised if nobody ever talks about how three Head Witches lost their titles on the same day," I commented. "I don't see that being forgotten in a hurry."

"You'd be surprised," said Robin. "I'm more concerned with the hunters. I'm sure Linda will step aside out of sheer embarrassment and let Arabella have her coven's base back, but it was Arabella who invited them in to begin with. The other witches won't let her forget that, at least."

"I just hope they leave Rebecca alone once she's set free." I heaved a sigh. "Her mother has done nothing but try to manipulate her ever since she was chosen as Head Witch, and between the hunters and the other Head

Witches, she's had almost no chance at a normal childhood."

"You'd think her age would have stopped her being picked," Robin said. "But we aren't the ones who set the rules."

"The sceptres are. I know." I glanced around at the other witches crowding in the garden. "There's nothing to stop Meredith's sceptre picking someone who might try the same thing again, and nobody has a problem with that?"

"I mean, the sceptres have some degree of autonomy," said Robin. "I can't speak to *morality*, but each sceptre definitely has a level of control over who it picks, even if it can't know what the person in question will do with the power they're given."

"Isn't there a way to stop the sceptre picking someone who's likely to use it to commit murder?"

"Aside from restricting who gets to try to pick it up to begin with?" asked Robin. "No, but the sceptres are supposed to be more ceremonial than anything, and we're not even expected to use them to cast spells except in self-defence. Certain people seem to have forgotten— What's going on over there?"

The sound of raised voices drifted from the house. At the top of the stone staircase, Catherine Oakley appeared to be arguing with Arabella Knotgrass, who stood in the doorway, barring the way into the house.

"What's happening?" Robin asked the nearest witch, Stephanie Underhill.

She looked even more sour than she had earlier, perhaps because Rebecca being set free had thwarted her chances of wielding the sceptre. If I were Rebecca, I'd have said she was welcome to it.

"Arabella is claiming that the sceptre has gone missing." Stephanie scowled. "Meredith's sceptre, that is."

"It rolled under the cabinet," I said. "It's missing?"

"Apparently so." She didn't sound convinced. "In her house. How convenient."

"I didn't steal the sceptre," Arabella protested loudly from the top of the stairs. "You're the ones who left it behind when you brought Meredith downstairs."

Uh-oh.

Catherine Oakley scoffed loudly. "You expect me to believe that?"

"Arabella, you're the owner of the cabinet." Madame Grey stepped between them. "What exactly is on the other side of the portal inside it?"

A chill raced down my spine. *A portal to Fairyland,* she'd said. Had the sceptre somehow disappeared inside? Or had someone come *out* of the portal and taken it? Arabella had been downstairs the whole time, unless her house had somehow moved the sceptre elsewhere.

Robin grabbed my arm, bringing my attention back to the garden. "It's Rebecca."

I spun towards the gate, momentarily forgetting about the argument on the stairs. Robin and I made our way over to meet Rebecca. Blythe stood in front of her, glowering at the other witches as if to make it clear she wouldn't forget the way they'd treated her.

I stepped past her and wrapped Rebecca in a hug. "I'm glad you're back."

"I knew you'd solve this," she mumbled into my shoulder. "Thanks, Blair."

"I nearly didn't." I released Rebecca and turned to her sister. "She's free? No catch?"

"None whatsoever," Blythe said. "The hunters still haven't taken the real killer into custody yet?"

"They will, but the witches are arguing again." I pointed up at the house. "Apparently, Meredith's sceptre went missing in the room with the cabinet. Did she ever mention anything else about what's inside it?"

"You know as much as I do." Blythe frowned at the house. "Meredith was fixated on it, though."

"Meredith was the real killer?" Rebecca asked. "Why?"

"I honestly don't know," I admitted. "She seemed to think she was proving a point about the Head Witches being corrupt, but Arabella claimed the cabinet contained a portal to Fairyland. How is that even possible?"

"A question we'll return to later," Madame Grey answered, sweeping in behind Rebecca as if to shield her from the others' judgement. "I intend to find out the details of how she obtained it, but if Meredith's sceptre has indeed been stolen, we have a more immediate issue on our hands."

"What happens when a sceptre goes missing?" I asked. "Can they vote in a new Head Witch for the region at all?"

"The leaders of the major local covens will have to either agree to be drawn under the influence of the Head Witch of another region or pick a Head Witch the old-fashioned way," said Madame Grey. "That is, with a vote and without a sceptre being involved. I don't see either option being popular."

"They're still within the rules," Blythe said. "I looked it up."

"It is," said Madame Grey. "But I've found most people are slow to let go of tradition, even to their own detriment."

"That is correct."

All eyes turned to the gate, where Aveline Hollyhock stood, as beaky-faced and imposing as ever. Her long-suffering daughter stood at her side, dressed in a long travelling cloak, but it was the former Head Witch who commanded the attention. A ripple of shock passed among the other witches, and even Catherine Oakley and the others stopped their argument.

Nearby, Stephanie Underhill took a startled step backwards. "What's she doing here?"

"I guess she heard." Rebecca eyed her predecessor with an expression of mild horror. Aveline had been furious to lose her title to a child and had immediately gone into retirement without ever checking in on Rebecca, so I doubted even Stephanie had ever expected to see her again. "Like everyone else."

"She can't have heard all of it." When I caught sight of Robin's bewildered expression, I added, "That's Aveline Hollyhock. Former Head Witch."

"Oh," she said. "Oh boy."

"Yeah. Better hope she came to stop a fight and not start one."

"How unexpected," Madame Grey said. "Aveline Hollyhock. To what do I owe the pleasure?"

"It's not you I'm here to see." Aveline hobbled through the throng of witches, leaning heavily on her walking stick, and halted at the foot of the staircase to survey the other Head Witches. "Pitiful. You're a disgrace to the title of Head Witch. Almost all of you are."

"What are you doing at my house?" Arabella demanded.

"Perhaps I simply came to pay my respects to the unfortunate lost Head Witches," Aveline said. "And to remind you to hand over their sceptres for safekeeping."

"It's Meredith Norwood's sceptre that's the problem," Catherine Oakley said. "It's missing."

"Well, that's inconvenient," said Aveline. "Who lost it?"

"It's somewhere in the house," said Jodie Atwater, who seemed determined not to acknowledge Rebecca's return. "We can't pick a replacement for Meredith without her sceptre."

"Untrue," said Aveline. "Personally, I'd be more inclined to break all your sceptres in two and be done with it, but nothing in the rules says the Head Witch has to carry a sceptre at all. I looked it up myself, since everyone seems to have neglected to study the actual rules in the past few hundred years."

"I know the rules inside and out," Jodie said, sounding affronted.

"Knowing the rules and obeying them are two entirely different things," said Aveline. "They also state that a Head Witch can be replaced at any time, if the other coven leaders agree, and can even resign her position by choice. Personally, I'd find it preferable to waiting for that Head Witch to die first, but that's not why I came here."

"Then why?" Arabella demanded of her. "You're not Head Witch any longer."

I spotted Stephanie nodding in agreement, though the motion stopped when Aveline cast a withering look in her direction.

"My successor was on the brink of being arrested for a crime she didn't commit, thanks to someone's decision to invite the hunters into their house," said Aveline. "I hope that mistake will not be repeated."

So did I. The hunters themselves were conspicuously absent at the moment. They knew they had no part in the witches' debate after all, though I did see Nathan and Erin standing next to Buck, Erin's fiancé.

"What would you have done?" Arabella asked. "Nobody here was unbiased."

"Including the hunters." Rebecca's voice rang out, and she gave the witches a glare that indicated she wouldn't forget the accusations in a hurry. "You know, I didn't know I was allowed to resign my title, but after all this, I'm tempted to. Who would want to be a part of this?"

Aveline chuckled. "She has more sense than the rest of you fools. We'll leave you to your arguments. Try not to kill anyone else."

"We?" echoed Rebecca. "We're not leaving."

"I think we've worn out our welcome," said Madame Grey. "Arabella is about a minute from throwing everyone out of her house, and the hunters have nothing more to say to us. Even Linda Graham."

"Please tell me she's going to resign her position," I said to her. "She can't be allowed to keep her authority after what she did."

"Don't worry." Nathan stepped up to my side. "She won't. Shall we go?"

Madame Grey swept out of the gates first, and the others took that as their cue to disperse. Stephanie Underhill all but fled before she could fall under the gaze of Aveline Hollyhock. I still didn't trust her not to have her own agenda concerning Rebecca's sceptre, but it was safe to say she hadn't expected her former rival to power to show up.

"Robin, come on," said Lady Wildwood.

"Just a second." Robin waved at Rebecca then me. "Nice meeting you."

Tansy squeaked in agreement.

"You too," I replied. "It's nice to know at least one other Head Witch has her head screwed on the right way round."

Robin grinned. Aveline Hollyhock seemed to find that amusing for some reason, and she chuckled as she hobbled out of the gates behind Madame Grey.

Blythe and Rebecca departed next, and Nathan and I followed. I was all too happy not to spend another minute in that house, despite my unsatisfied curiosity about that portal to Fairyland—and how Arabella had obtained it.

In the end, a larger part of me just wanted to go home with Nathan.

He fell into step with me as we left the house behind, his hand sliding into mine. "I wish we didn't have to go straight home. After that, I think we deserve a holiday."

"I have a feeling this is only the start." I looked back at the large, grand house and the fences surrounding its gardens and wondered if there were other reasons the coven had picked such a distant place to set up their base. "That missing sceptre... where'd it go? Or should I be asking, who took it?"

He squeezed my hand. "I'm not going to be able to convince you it isn't your problem, am I?"

"You know me better than that." I studied his face. "I know I'm not Head Witch, but she said *Fairyland*. My dad is going to want to know. I can't keep that from him."

"I know," he said. "I'd just prefer for us not to be drawn into the Head Witches' squabbles over how to pick a replacement."

"We won't... not directly," I said. "It's not my region, after all, but I hope Rebecca gets a break for a bit. Though I have a feeling I'm about to be replaced as her mentor."

"Aveline will probably have to go through Blythe first," said Nathan. "You can leave the mentoring to her for a bit while we spend a little time together, can't you?"

"Define 'a little.'" I tilted my head to one side. "You still have that holiday time saved up, right?"

"Yes, and since the meeting was cut short, it seems a pity

to go straight back to work." He leaned in to hug me, and a grin swept across my face.

"Okay, you've convinced me." I kissed him on the lips. "Where do you want to go?"

This might be the last bit of peace the two of us had for a while, given the changes about to sweep across the magical world and the ripples they'd leave in their wake. The witches, as was clear, weren't good with change. Neither were the hunters, especially the ones who favoured their own advancement over the good of the community, but both were about to face a reckoning. As were the rest of us, but we could weather that storm, like we had so many others.

One thing was certain. Nathan and I would never have secrets between us again, not if I could help it.

ABOUT THE AUTHOR

Elle Adams lives in the middle of England, where she spends most of her time reading an ever-growing mountain of books, planning her next adventure, or writing. Elle's books are humorous mysteries with a paranormal twist, packed with magical mayhem.

She also writes urban and contemporary fantasy novels as Emma L. Adams.

Visit http://www.elleadamsauthor.com/ to find out more about Elle's books.